Written in the Stars

WITHDRAWN

AISHA SAEED

Nancy Paulsen Books

An Imprint of Penguin Group (USA)

NANCY PAULSEN BOOKS
Published by the Penguin Group
Penguin Group (USA) LLC
375 Hudson Street
New York, NY 10014

USA | Canada | UK | Ireland | Australia
New Zealand | India | South Africa | China
penguin.com
A Penguin Random House Company

Library of Congress Cataloging-in-Publication Data
is available upon request.

Printed in the United States of America.
ISBN 978-0-399-17170-3
1 3 5 7 9 10 8 6 4 2

Design by Richard Amari.
Text set in Lapidary333.
The publisher does not have any control over and does not assume
any responsibility for third-party websites or their content.

PUBLISHER'S NOTE
This is a work of fiction. Names, characters, places, and incidents
either are the product of the author's imagination or are used
fictitiously, and any resemblance to actual persons, living or dead,
businesses, companies, events, or locales is entirely coincidental.

To every Naila everywhere

Part One

Chapter 1

Naila, I wish you didn't have to miss the game," Carla tells me.

"Game?" I check the road, on the lookout for my mom, before turning to her. She rolls her eyes, her blond hair up in its cheerleader ponytail. Our lives may have changed a lot since we met in first grade, but that eye roll with the annoyed pout, that hasn't changed at all.

"Game?" She looks at Eric. "Do you believe her? It's only the last game of Saif's high school career." She turns to me. "Naila, are you really going to miss this one too?"

"You know I can't go."

"It's his last game, Naila."

I glance back at Saif. He's wearing his blue soccer jersey and chatting with a friend a safe distance away by the green mosaic mural next to our high school's entrance. I take in his lean frame, his olive skin, and the brown hair that brushes against his eyes. He catches my eye just then;

his dimple deepens with his smile. He takes a step toward us, and then stops, remembering why he can't approach.

"See?" Carla exhales. "He knows he can't even stand here with us because your parents might freak out."

"My mom might freak out if she sees Eric standing here too," I remind her, jabbing a finger toward the road.

"I still don't get it," she continues. "He's the sweetest boyfriend ever. Any parent should be thankful their daughter met a guy like him. What's their deal?"

I've explained it all to her too many times. I'm starting to think she just doesn't want to hear it. "It's complicated," I finally say.

"Well, you know what's not complicated?" she counters. "That he's the most understanding guy I've ever met. Seriously, Eric"—she touches his arm—"would we be celebrating our three-month anniversary next week if I never so much as stepped past this curb with you?"

Eric clears his throat. "Um, good question, but"—he glances back—"I think Saif's calling me, so, uh, I'll leave you both to discuss that." He kisses Carla and jogs over to Saif.

Good, I think, relaxing a little now that I am alone with Carla.

"I want to go tonight, Carla," I tell her. "You know I do, but my parents—"

"Oh, come on!" Carla shakes her head. "They can't keep you locked up forever. Just sneak out the window. Just this once! You're not twelve years old. Besides, your parents zonk out by nine o'clock anyways. I can pick you up. At least you'll catch the last half. It would mean so much to him."

"I wish I could, but I can't. We'll be in college this time next year. I can't risk getting caught now."

I don't mention the tension that's built between my parents ever since I got my acceptance letter last week or the hushed arguments about whether or not I will go away to college at all.

"Hey," Saif calls out to Carla, "Eric and I are leaving without you if you don't hurry up!"

"Fine." Carla rolls her eyes at me again. "You can't say I didn't try."

She walks over to join Saif and Eric. Before they all head to the student parking lot, Saif turns to look at me. *Love you,* I mouth to him. I press my palm to my lips and blow him a silent kiss. He grins—and then they disappear behind the curve.

Only now does my jaw unclench, my shoulders relax. And only now do I let myself acknowledge that familiar mixture of relief and guilt that has been my companion this past year.

Has it already been a year? I think back. Yes. It's been one year since Saif told me he cared about me as more than just his friend. It's been one year since I told him I felt the same way and kissed him in the side courtyard with the tangled palm trees next to the library, deciding it was time to let my heart, and not fear, dictate what I would do. And—my stomach tightens—it's been one year since I began deceiving my parents without ever once opening my mouth.

I hear a honk. My mother's minivan pulls up to the curb.

"Sorry, beta, I had to stop and get gas," she says when I get inside. Her hair, more black than gray, is tied up in a loose bun; a large red scarf circles her neck despite today's exceptionally hot Florida sun. "I didn't realize I was this late, though." She scans the empty school entrance. "You should have stayed inside until you saw my car—you never know who is out there."

"Carla was here," I tell her quickly. "She only just left."

"She's a good girl." My mother smiles. "I'm glad you're both still friends."

"Well," I begin, "she was telling me about a soccer game tonight. She really wants me to go and support the team too. The school year's almost over, and all our friends are going to be there, and, well, we'll be room-mates in a few months anyways, so I was wondering—"

"No." My mother shoots me a surprised look. "You know that."

"But, Ami—" I begin.

"It's not you I'm worried about. It's all the boys that would be there. Besides, Auntie Lubna is having a party tonight. Did you forget already?"

"Is Imran going?" I bite my lip, knowing the answer.

"He has to study," she responds.

"Why can Imran skip these parties but I never can?"

"What's gotten into you today?" My mother glances at me. "If you don't go, people will wonder. You know how they talk. Besides, your brother gets bored. He doesn't have anyone his own age at these things. I already ironed your salwar kamiz. We'll leave as soon as your abu can shut down the dry cleaning business for the day."

I lean back into the seat. I've gone to more of my parents' dinner parties than I can count. Gatherings of their friends, all Pakistani immigrants like themselves, who meet almost every week at one another's homes to talk in the language they grew up with and listen to the music of their childhood.

I used to even eye Saif from afar at these dinner parties, until his sister Jehan got married to someone who shocked the entire community. His name was Justin. They didn't know much about him, except that he was definitely not Pakistani.

We all saw it coming, my mother had said in a horrified voice on the phone to her sister. *They never had any control over their kids. What else do you expect?*

I think my mother and her friends might have forgiven them this marriage had Saif's parents seemed remorseful about Jehan marrying outside the South Asian community. But they didn't seem ashamed at all.

No one invites them anymore.

I watch the trees along the road fly by as we drive past. It's almost summertime. Not that anyone can tell. Elsewhere there are seasons. Leaves bloom green and then turn gold and crimson as they fall to the earth, change coming to everything in its path.

Not here.

In my world, the leaves stay green, the same Florida heat beating down on us, day after day, year after year. Unchanging.

But not for long. Soon things will change. Soon they will have to. I've spent my entire life banking on this very truth.

Chapter 2

*W*hen we get home from dinner, I sit on the edge of the carpeted stairs and strain to hear my parents discuss me in the family room below.

"She could commute if she took classes two days a week," my mother says.

"Mehnaz, the university is two hours away."

"But she's too young! I can't help but worry."

"She's a smart girl. We have to trust we raised her right."

"What if she went to the community college here for the first two years? There's no harm in that. Maybe in the meantime, we'll find a good proposal for her and she can get married. Don't look at me like that. It's true. Many girls get married and continue their education. Which, by the way"—my mother pauses—"Shaista called today."

I grip the wooden bars of the railing. Not this. Not again.

"Mehnaz, we've already settled this." My father's voice lowers.

"Why don't you listen to me? Shaista said it is a very good proposal. He's doing his residency. Proposals like this don't come around every day. Naila would be taken care of for life. We should at least meet them."

"Do you know how difficult it is to get into the six-year medical program? Imran struggles with basic algebra, but Naila? She's brilliant. She's worked too hard to get there. She can wait and get married later."

I exhale. My father wanted to be a doctor once. I know he would never let my own dream go unfulfilled.

"Fine," my mother says. "You're probably right. I guess it's a mother's job to worry."

The sofa shifts below, and then, footsteps. I leap to my feet and dash to my room. Grabbing the closest textbook to me, I fling myself on my bed.

"Naila?"

My mother steps inside and sits down on the wicker chair by my bed. She's still wearing her blue salwar kamiz from the dinner party we went to—a long tunic with loose trousers and a scarf draped loosely around her shoulders. She normally wears her hair wrapped up in a bun, but looking at her now, the way it flows long and wavy past her shoulders, I see why people say I look just like her.

She glances around my bedroom and then closes her eyes for a moment. The pink textured wallpaper my father pasted up when I was born still looks new, as does the whitewashed furniture, despite a few scruffs and scratches from years ago. When she finally opens her eyes and looks at me, her eyes are wet.

"I can't begin to tell you how much I'm going to miss you."

"Ami." I sit up and move closer to her. "I'm not going far away."

"But, Naila"—she leans closer to me—"don't forget everything we've talked about. You're a beautiful girl, and there will be many who will like you."

"Not this again," I mumble. I try pulling away, but her hands grip my wrists.

"Don't look at me like that. It's true," my mother tells me. "Remember, just because you will be away at college doesn't mean the promises you've made no longer apply. You can choose many things," she continues. "You can choose what you want to be when you grow up, the types of shoes you want to buy, how long you want your hair to be. But your husband, that's different. We choose your husband for you. You understand that, right?"

I've heard this more times than I can count. The first time we had this conversation was seven years ago, when I was ten. "What if I find him first?" I asked then.

"That's not how it's done," she had said. "Just because we live in a different place doesn't change how things should be."

"But didn't you *want* to talk to Abu? Didn't you feel afraid?"

"My parents knew it was a good match, and they were right. You've seen others, your third cousin Roohi, who chose not to listen. Look at her now, divorced with young children. Her parents can't even leave their home without hanging their heads in shame. Who wants to marry her now? A life of loneliness is an awful punishment for one bad decision. We don't want that for you. Trust us. Promise you won't disappoint us."

I watch my mother now. She twists her shawl with her fingers. I hate keeping secrets from her. But how can I explain that I see the world a little differently and my way of looking at the world isn't bad, not if it means their daughter has found someone she loves, someone who makes her completely and unbelievably happy?

I want to tell her all of this. But I know I can't. At least not yet.

"Ami." I look at her, giving her the reassurance she came for. "Trust me, I won't disappoint you."

Chapter 3

The next morning, I find my father and Imran sitting at the kitchen table poring over a booklet.

"What's going on?"

Imran looks up and grins, his brown curls poking through his baseball cap. "Abu's showing me this driving manual! He's going to teach me!"

"Driving manual?" I repeat. "But Imran isn't even fifteen yet."

My father shrugs. "You know your brother and cars. It's about time he learned to drive one."

"When do you think I'll learn?" I ask. "I'm seventeen. I'm probably the only person in my class who can't drive yet."

"What's the rush?" my father asks. "Ami's schedule works perfectly to take you to and from school, and you don't need a car in college."

I look at both of them. I should argue with my father like I normally would, but today I don't want to. Maybe it's because I know that by this time next year I'll be in college with Saif and Carla, and that helps this injustice sting less.

"That's great," I tell them. And somehow it is.

I find Saif at our usual spot in the courtyard at lunch. He's standing by our gray picnic table looking down at his phone. A touch of sun reflects against his brown hair, making it look almost golden. He looks up and smiles at me.

"Hey, you, what's going on?" I grin, approaching him.

"You are." He puts his arms around my waist and draws me close. "You're what's going on."

I laugh and trace the slight stubble around his jaw and kiss him. We have two classes together, but this, right here, is the only time we have all to ourselves. I live for these thirty-five minutes.

"Look." I sit down next to him and pull out my phone. "Carla sent this to me last night. You were amazing."

I rest my head on his chest. His arm drapes around my shoulders. I show him the video—she sends them all the time. Brief snippets of the moments I miss. But this one is extra special. I smile as I watch it again. Saif dribbling the soccer ball. Saif scoring the game-winning goal.

"So that's why she was staring at her cell phone the whole night," he says.

"I just wish I could have been there to see it myself."

"It's okay." He shrugs. "There's always college, right? Speaking of which . . ." He looks down at me. "Did your parents say anything more to you?"

"Well." I sit up and look at him. "Last night, actually, my mom talked to me and finally, officially, said yes!"

"I knew it!" He pulls me close, hugging me tightly. I wrap my arms around his neck, hugging him back.

"I can't believe it. I mean, I can, but now it just feels a little more real. And you know what? I will be sitting front and center for all your games in just a few months. I'm never going to miss another game again."

He pulls out his lunch and grins at me. "I was so hoping they'd say yes. Now we can finally breathe."

"And bonus?" I tell him. "I can start counting down the dinners I have to go to with my parents starting this Saturday. I can't wait to finally start doing what I'd like with my weekends."

I expect him to be happy, but he stares down at the turkey sandwich in his lap.

"What's wrong?"

"It's nothing." He smiles at me, but I notice his eyes don't crinkle with the upturn of his lips.

"It's something," I insist. "You know you can tell me anything."

"I know." He takes my hand and holds it in his. It's a habit. Something he does whenever we're about to talk about something that's not easy. Whenever he wants to remind me, without having to say a word, that no matter what it is, it's not enough to change anything between us.

But right now it worries me.

"It's not a big deal." He finally shrugs. "It's just, well, you mentioned Saturday, and I got a little bummed because Saturday is prom and all. I know you can't go"—he squeezes my hand—"and it's okay. It's fine. I'll go stag like I do every year, but you know, they booked the Brinks Hotel, right off the water, everyone just keeps talking about it and going on and on, and I just keep thinking, man, it would have been nice to take the smartest, prettiest girl in school to this one final prom."

I've been tuning out the chatter about prom. I knew I couldn't go, so why get fixated? But I had no idea until this moment that it might matter to him. I grip his hand tighter.

"I'm sorry." I look down. "I feel like a broken record. You know I want to go. But my parents . . ." I trail off. The words have been said so many times, they feel like sand in my mouth. I'm tired of always giving him these same reasons. These same excuses for missing out on the important milestones in our lives. I swallow back tears.

"I just don't get it. Why do your parents hate me so much?"

"You know that's not true. It's not you. They'd hate anyone I was dating, because I'm not allowed to date. It has nothing to do with you."

"I've heard the gossip, though," he says. "Apparently my sister ruined our family name by running off with some guy she barely knew, and me? Well, I'm too busy playing sports to ever amount to much of anything." He looks at my stricken face and nods. "Yep, thought so. And my parents? They don't know how to control their kids. Does that about cover it?"

"Don't listen to them." My eyes fill with tears. "Their words don't make any of it true, do they? I love your parents. I love you. I know the truth. Isn't that what matters?"

"It matters what your parents think of me, Naila. If they're ever going to accept us, it matters."

"They will accept us one day," I insist. "And when they do, they're going to see what I see. They'll love you too. They don't get it right now. They think there's only one way to do things because it's all they ever knew, but they're not bad people, Saif. They can be reasoned with. One day we'll show them there's another way to look at all of this. I wasn't exactly planning to fall for you. I just did. It's going to happen to them too."

"Oh, yeah?" He laughs now.

"Cupid is staking out the house as we speak." I grin. "And maybe this time next year, they'll be telling me how awesome this Saif boy I found really is."

"Well, at least in a few months we won't have to sneak around anymore." He puts his arm around me. "We'll get dorm rooms near each other. Take all the same classes."

"Oh, yeah? The girls' dorm my parents are going to make sure I get? Will you be sneaking into my medical classes too?"

"Yep." He smiles. Our foreheads touch. I smell the sweetness of his breath and then he kisses me. It's been a year, but every time still feels like the first time.

"We'll make it work," I whisper.

"I know," he says. "And, hey, don't listen to me. It's only prom. Not the end of the world."

Still, I can't get Saif's crestfallen expression out of my head for the rest of the day. Suddenly it feels like all anyone can talk about is prom. Everywhere I turn, people are exchanging photos, debating shoe colors, and bragging about the kind of stretch limo their boyfriends rented for the night.

Even Carla is talking about it when I stand with her at the curb waiting for my mom to pick me up.

"Remember the red dress I told you about?" she asks. "I changed my mind. Look at this one." She hands me her phone. "Look at the straps on it. It's an exact match for my shoes! I nearly died. Naila? What's wrong? Oh, no." She looks at me. "Are you crying?"

"I'm not." I wipe away my tears. "I just . . . Saif really wanted to go. I know we'll be together soon, but this is prom. It meant a lot to him."

"Aw." Carla hugs me. "It's okay. You know they have homecoming dances and stuff in college too."

"Yeah." I clear my throat. "But it's prom. The last one." I shake my head and force a laugh. "Now I sound like you! It'll be fine. I'm just getting worked up for no reason."

She looks at the road, and suddenly her eyes light up. "Your mom is coming." She points to the minivan careening toward us. She leans into my ear and whispers, "Naila. You are going to love me."

"Carla! No!" I call out, but she's already ten steps ahead of me. Before I can say another word, the passenger window of my mother's car rolls down and Carla leans in.

"Hi, Mrs. R!" Carla exclaims. "Guess what? Saturday

is my birthday! We're not doing anything special, really, but my mom is making a cake and we're ordering in Chinese food, and it would mean *so* much if Naila could be there and spend the night. I know, I know, she's not allowed—I'm her best friend, so I know." She laughs. "But if you could make an exception just this once. I have a bunch of magazines on decorating our dorm I've been saving up since middle school, and I need Naila's input. We'll be roommates soon enough anyways. Please? Pretty please?"

There is a long pause. I wait for my mother to sternly tell me to get in the car. To see through everything Carla is trying to do.

The pause is interminable. And then my ears start playing tricks on me.

"No boys will be there, right?"

"Well, my brother"—she laughs—"but he's seven, so hopefully that's okay."

"Okay," my mother finally says. "It sounds like fun."

Carla moves aside. I walk past her. I can't look at her, much less process what just happened.

I get in the car and stare at my mother when she says, "Maybe it's time for me to start practicing how it will be when you're not here anymore."

She smiles at me, and I feel something much like hope

swimming through me. She didn't want me to go away to college. But I'm going. She has never let me spend the night at Carla's, but today she said yes. Maybe there is hope.

Maybe the things I told Saif were true.

My parents will eventually come around.

It's only a matter of time . . .

Chapter 4

"What are you doing?"

I jump at the sound of Imran's voice. He's standing by my bedroom door, watching me with barely concealed laughter.

"What?" I shrug. "Carla's almost here. I'm just straightening my hair."

"You never straighten your hair. Finally trying to look like a girl?"

I give him a playful shove. "How about you stick to being my brother and not my sister? If I need fashion advice, I'll ask."

"Seriously, though," he says. "It's pretty cool Ami's letting you hang out with Carla."

"I think you were barely out of diapers the last time that happened," I tell him.

"You know what this means, right? Ami has really accepted you're going away to college." He looks down. "It's going to be so weird when you're gone."

"Are you going to miss me?" I grin. "No more banging on the door for the bathroom, no one complaining the music is too loud for her to study."

"Yeah, that stuff will be pretty awesome." He smiles and looks at me. "But I'm still going to miss you."

I feel a lump in my throat and give him a hug. "I'll miss you too."

I watch him leave and then look at myself in the mirror. The straightener did its magic. My hair falls straight and soft against my shoulders. My cheeks are tinged pink. I feel slightly flushed.

Nerves? I wonder.

Or is it guilt?

"Oh. My. God. Naila. Is this really happening?" Carla greets me when I get into her car with my overnight bag.

"I can't believe it," she continues. "If there were Olympic medals for best friends, I'd be getting the gold, right? I can't believe it worked!" She looks at me and frowns. "Why aren't you pounding the dashboard with giddiness? Why do you look like we're heading to a funeral?"

I shake my head. "I don't know. It's the first time I ever flat-out lied to them."

The car slows as we approach a red light. She turns to me. "Okay, yeah, that sucks. But listen, you can't let that get you down tonight. You want to sulk about it later and figure out what it means, I'll be there to work out all the ways you feel awful about this, but tonight? Tonight is going to be special, and you won't ever have a chance to experience it again."

She's right. I know she is. And somehow, just like that, the burden lifts. Tonight, Saif is going to take me to prom. Tonight, this is all that matters.

I lay my suitcase on her bed and pull out my outfit. Carla's dress hangs by her closet, the slinky, strappy dress cut just above the knee. I look at mine. My traditional Pakistani dress seemed beautiful at home. I run my hand over the fragile silk floor-length gown with hand-stitched ivory beads and pink flowering tulle along the edges, sent by my aunt in Pakistan. It's pretty, but compared to Carla's dress, it's not exactly going to fit in.

My phone blinks. It's Saif. *What color is your dress?*

Well, pink, I type out, *but it's sort of . . . not a dress? I'm wearing a lengha. Just warning you! Promise you'll still go with me? ;)*

I rest the phone on the dresser, waiting for the fast response he usually gives me. But this time it's silent. He's busy getting ready too, I tell myself.

I sit on the white kitchen stool Carla dragged into the bedroom. She pokes at my eyes, her hands fluttering with the makeup brush. "Sit still." She exhales. "I swear it's like working on a five-year-old."

"You're tickling me." I laugh.

Finally, she's done. I take a look in the mirror and gasp at the person looking back at me. Aside from lip gloss, I never wear makeup, but right now, with the shimmering eye shadow, the eyeliner, the mascara—

"Oh, my gosh. I'm a princess. You made me into a princess," I whisper.

"Yep." Carla grins. "Future makeup artist to the stars."

"More like my fairy godmother." I hug her.

"Okay, don't mess up my makeup now," Carla says, but she's laughing, and hugs me back. "You look so pretty, Naila. The outfit totally works. I'm so excited for you."

The doorbell rings in the distance.

They're here.

Carla's mother knocks on the door and pokes her head in just as Carla laces up her strappy heels. "Beautiful. Both of you!" she gushes. And then—my eyes are blinded by a flash.

"Sorry." Carla grabs my arm. "I forgot to warn you, my parents just got their newest camera, and they're slightly obsessed."

But Carla's protestations over the brightness of the flash and being photographed keep me distracted from a tiny worry that has crept in and is growing as we get closer to the living room: Saif never texted me back.

The fear vanishes once I see him.

Because there is Saif. His smile, the smile I love, is breaking into a grin when he sees me. But—I stare at him again—he's not wearing the tux he sent me a photo of earlier that morning. Instead, he's wearing a fitted black sherwani. I take in the silver embroidered cuffs, the handwork on the collar. It's more stylish than anything my brother or father have ever worn to a Pakistani wedding or special event, but it's a sherwani.

"But you rented a tux . . ." I walk up to him, running a hand over his sleeve. "You did this for me?"

"Had to coordinate with my girl." He grins. "Look okay?"

"Looks amazing," I say, trying not to cry.

"Here." He opens a box, and inside is a delicate pink rose tied with a cream ribbon. He holds my hand, tying the corsage around my wrist.

We step out onto the lawn for photos, and everything feels tinged with a gentle starry haze. The black stretch limo and waiting driver. I am aware there is a world out there, real and tangible, but all that matters in this moment is Saif.

"We'll catch up with you guys in a minute," Saif tells Carla and Eric when we arrive at the hotel. He takes my hand, and we make our way to the boardwalk overlooking the ocean.

"You look beautiful," Saif whispers in my ear. As he stands behind me, his face brushes against mine as his arms wrap around me. I turn to look at him. He's looking at me so intently, so intensely, I can't breathe. And then his lips are on mine, and I know life can't possibly get better than this.

At the hotel I take in the ornate chandeliers, gold ceilings, and the classical music in the lobby before we enter the hall. It's like we landed in a fairy tale.

We get compliments. I'm certain we give some too. Speeches are given. A king and queen are announced, but I can't focus on any of it. All I see is Saif.

On the dance floor, I wrap my arms around him and rest my head on his shoulder as a slower song begins. The dance floor is packed with people, but the rotating lights flickering through the room make me feel like we're enclosed in our own canopy together.

"I don't want this night to end," I tell him.

"That's good." He pulls me closer. "Because we just got started. You may not have known this about me, but I kind of love to dance."

"Um, I think my feet already got that message loud and clear." I laugh. "You may have to carry me to the limo at the end of the night." I lean up and kiss him.

He doesn't kiss me back.

27

He's stopped dancing altogether.

I look up at him. He's staring at something just over my shoulder. Some of our friends have stopped dancing too, though the music continues playing. They are all looking in the same direction. I follow Saif's shocked expression.

And then I see.

My parents.

They are standing three feet away on this very dance floor—my mother in a gray cotton salwar kamiz, smudged kohl around her eyes. My father, brown sandals on his feet, his pepper-gray hair in disarray.

For a moment no one speaks. Then I hear Saif's voice. "Can we talk?" He clears his throat and does his best to appear calm. "Outside? It might be a good idea if we all just go outside and talk about this."

My mother takes a step toward us, and only then do I realize how tightly I'm holding Saif's hand. With one fluid motion, she slaps my hand from his and grabs my wrist.

"Please," Saif says. "If we all could talk. Just for a second."

"Don't." She glares at him. "Don't you dare speak to me. Ever."

I look at my father. He's not really looking at me. More like through me.

My mother's grip is tighter now. She's pulling me off the dance floor. Toward the door. I look back at Saif. His face has gone pale. He walks toward me. I shake my head at him.

"Ami," I whisper, though choked sobs, "if you could just listen to us. If we could just step outside and talk for even five minutes and explain to you what's going on."

"I think the explanation is clear enough," she responds. "And now let me explain something to you, Naila. It's over."

Chapter 5

The pale moon shines on us as we get into the car. The ride home is silent, but it's a heavy silence, closing in on me. I feel like I'm suffocating.

"I'm sorry," Imran says once we're inside the house. His hands are in his pockets. His face is stained with tears. "I got a text. It was a photo. From Omar—you know him, right? And then someone else sent me the same picture. And then it was like over and over again, the same photo of you from all different people. I wasn't going to let Ami know," he insists, "but she heard the pings and grabbed it from me and . . . " His voice trails off. "I didn't mean to get you in trouble."

"Imran." My mother glares at him. "Go to your room. Now."

"I'm so, so sorry." His voice grows small.

I try to process Imran's words, but before I can, my father's silence explodes into rage.

"Boyfriend?" he yells. "My daughter has a boyfriend?" His words reverberate through the house. They shake the walls.

I shudder. *Boyfriend* is a dirty, shameful word.

But Saif isn't my boyfriend. He's Saif. The boy who brings me my favorite granola bars and teases me relentlessly, until my sides ache from laughter.

"Guess who called us on the way over to collect you?" He looks at my mother. "Shela's mother, Balkis. Shela's your classmate, remember? Didn't you stop and think that someone might see you there? Everyone is talking about us now. They're laughing at us. How can we ever show our face anywhere again?"

My mother reaches for a napkin to dab her eyes.

I think of Balkis. How many times has she visited my mother with a smile on her face as she leans in and whispers about someone's son or daughter, or rumors of discord in the house of a mutual acquaintance? I imagine her in someone else's house, her ears and neck draped with gold, sipping tea and pouring forth all my secrets.

I want to tell them all about Shela and point out the obvious: Shela was at prom too. I know her secrets just as she's known mine. I open my mouth to settle the score, but my father speaks first.

"Your mother and I have discussed this matter." He

lifts my laptop from the coffee table and tucks it under his arm. "And we've come to a few decisions. The first decision is the business with this boy is over. You will not see him again."

I look down at the floor.

"The second thing, no more school."

"But"—tears fill my eyes—"school's almost over."

My father adjusts his glasses. "It seems you weren't worried about school when you decided to take this family's reputation and run it through the mud. Of all the people in the world." He draws a sharp intake of breath. "That boy? That family? I don't know what kind of spell he cast over you to make you break every promise you ever made to us."

I flinch at his words as though he had slapped me.

"I gave you so much. I trusted you." His voice breaks. "Now you're going to have to trust me."

Chapter 6

The next day, Imran is the only one who will speak to me. That night he sneaks me his phone when our parents are asleep. Over the noise of his stereo, I whisper to Saif in Imran's closet.

"What if I tried to talk to your parents again?" Saif asks. "My mom could come too. Maybe having another adult there might help."

"It wouldn't work. They're so angry, Saif. I've never seen them this way. They won't even look at me."

"But I have to explain myself to them." His voice brightens. "I know! Graduation is Wednesday. My parents can approach them. Force them to discuss the situation."

"I don't think I'm going to my graduation."

"But you're the salutatorian! They're expecting you to speak."

"I heard my mother talking about it with my father."

"I can't believe this," he mutters.

"I don't know what to do, Saif. The phone keeps ringing. People won't stop calling to ask if the rumors are true. I don't know how to fix this," I whisper.

"Naila, I love you. Nothing's changed. Look, either we give in, or they do. I'm not giving up. Are you? We need a plan, but sooner or later it'll work out. It has to."

His words stay with me the next day. They linger in my thoughts as I watch my mother in the kitchen. Her mouth remains set in a thin straight line, devoid of emotion. It's as if I'm a stranger. I've tried apologizing, explaining, but my words are weightless, floating away unheard.

But that doesn't mean I stop trying. I should at least try to talk to her, help her understand what happened, why I did what I did.

I look at the wall clock—my father won't be home for another few hours. I step into the kitchen and watch her place the teakettle on the stove. She is wearing a burnt orange salwar kamiz. Her hair is up in its usual bun. I hear the clicking sound of the gas stove as it ignites. She sits down with a newspaper, her face obscured.

"Ami?"

Silence.

"Ami, I need to talk to you."

The paper rustles as she turns a page. I hesitate for a moment before plunging in.

"Ami, I'm sorry. I will never forgive myself for lying to you. But Saif, he's not a bad person. This wasn't his fault. Maybe he could come by with his mother?"

"No," comes a quiet but firm voice from behind the paper veil. My mother lowers the newspaper and looks directly at me. I feel a sinking sensation.

"Have you been speaking with him?"

My heart begins to pound. "No." I look down at the floor.

She's silent for a long time before she speaks again, and when she does, her voice is harder than I've ever heard it before. "You let him know I'm not taking phone calls. I'm not having guests over, and I'm not talking to him. Or his mother." Her voice lowers with a tone of finality. "Don't ask me again."

The kettle begins to whistle. I watch her stand up. She tucks the newspaper under her arm and walks out the room, taking with her all the hope I had.

Chapter 7

From my bedroom that evening I hear my parents in the kitchen speaking in hushed voices. My stomach clenches. Are they talking about me? My graduation? My going away to college?

Carefully I make my way down the stairs. As though sensing my presence, my mother turns around.

"Beta." She motions with her hand for me to join them.

She called me beta. And the way she said it, as though I am her daughter again.

I feel myself choking up with gratitude. Maybe Saif is right. Maybe things are going to be okay.

My mother looks at my father, who is looking off toward the window. He grips his cell phone in his hands. "Your father and I discussed everything that happened," she says.

I tense and glance at my father. He still won't look at me.

"We came to one conclusion," she continues. "This was our fault. How can we blame you for your sins when we did not teach you well enough?"

What?

"We always meant to take you and Imran to Pakistan every year," she continues. "If we had, this would never have happened. We've talked about it at great length, and we've made a decision. We're going to go for a visit to Pakistan. Our flight is Wednesday."

"Wednesday," I repeat, looking at both of them in confusion. "Which Wednesday?"

"This Wednesday."

Cold beads of sweat form on my forehead. Wednesday is only two days away. It's my graduation day.

"So soon?" I swallow back tears.

Ami nods toward Abu's cell phone. "We already booked our tickets."

"But, Ami, Abu," I tell them, "if we delayed it just a week, I could go to my graduation and have time to get ready. And besides—"

My father interrupts, "Were we supposed to consult you? Like you consulted with us before you made a decision that has ruined all of us?"

"Imtiaz, there's no need to get into this right now." Ami presses a hand on his shoulder.

"No." He shrugs off her hand. "No. She needs to

know." He looks directly at me now. "Do you know why the phone won't stop ringing? Do you know just how many taunts we get?"

"Imtiaz," my mother whispers.

"Look at your mother," he shouts. "Look at your mother! Didn't you think for one minute, Naila? Didn't you realize you would get caught? That word would spread? Everyone knows. Here is your poor mother, telling everyone how good her daughter is, what good character she has. Now she is the fool."

My throat constricts.

"You were my pride and joy. I trusted you completely." His voice cracks. "Now where will we ever find a respectable match for you?"

"Abu," I plead, "maybe you don't have to make a match for me. Maybe things can be different. Just because it's different doesn't automatically make it bad. I don't—"

My father slams his hand on the countertop. "Do you hear her? We thought we raised her well, but listen to her." He looks directly at me. "We had such high hopes for you. We supported you. It was just one thing, the only thing, we asked you not to do—and now? Now everyone knows we failed. Even worse, we know we failed."

I swallow and look down at my feet. I am too frightened to cry.

"I know it's sudden." My mother rests a hand on my shoulder. "But I think we need a change of scenery. This has been very difficult for all of us. Maybe if we go back for a visit, you can understand us a bit more. Besides, you'll be in college soon. When else will we have a chance to visit Pakistan for one month like this?"

She said college.

I look at her. They're going to let me go. They even planned the trip for a month so I'd be back in time for orientation.

I take a proper breath, my first in ages. Maybe one month away will do some good. Maybe a month is what we all need to decompress, away from phone calls and pointed glances. Maybe one month will help them to be more open to the things I need them to understand. Maybe a vacation to Pakistan is the best possible solution there is.

Chapter 8

The plane speeds off the runway, gliding gracefully into flight. I look at my mother sitting next to me. She is already asleep. All around me, people are dozing, quiet, steady snores escaping their mouths.

I flip through the magazine in my lap, but can't focus. My thoughts continue to lead me elsewhere, traveling back to the night before.

I had flinched as I slid open my creaky bedroom window, praying my parents slept soundly. I had to see Saif and decided it was worth the risk. I couldn't leave without saying good-bye. I stepped into the grassy forest behind our house. I heard nothing but silence.

Finally I saw Saif at the edge of the forest, and we followed the small sandy trail deep into the woods.

"My dad said we're staying with his brother, my chacha. It's a small village. I'm not sure if they even have Internet," I told him. "The phones aren't reliable, and I don't want to risk getting caught, so I don't know how I'll be able to contact you while I'm there."

"I had a feeling that might be the case," Saif said. His small flashlight shot a bolt of light through the dark night, and I saw his face, his eyes crinkled in a smile. "Here," he said, giving me a plastic bag.

"What's this?" Putting my hand inside, I felt something small and cool to the touch—a cell phone.

"I bought it this morning. It's pretty basic, but it has an international SIM card. You can text with it too."

Relief flowed through me. As usual, Saif came through. Just like that, he made the upcoming month feel considerably less daunting. Despite the ocean that would soon separate us, he would remain just a text away. I slipped the thin phone into my back pocket and hugged him one last time.

Chapter 9

Stepping off the plane, I wade through the people surrounding me, trailing behind my parents until finally we are out of the security gates and into the main airport terminal.

The number of people I see is staggering. Some of the women are in traditional salwar kamizes. Others are in head coverings and flowing dark burkas that sweep the ground with each step. I pass two women with streaked blond hair in jeans and T-shirts, talking animatedly on cell phones as a stream of men walk past in salwar kamizes in shades of beige, white, and gray. Some sport large, thick mustaches; others are clean shaven in dark black suits and crisp collared shirts, carrying leather briefcases.

Suddenly I hear a loud cry in the distance. My mother looks up, and her face breaks into a smile. "They're here! Can you believe it?" She tugs at my father's elbow. "Almost everyone came."

I follow my mother's gaze, and then I see them: a group

in the distance, twenty people, maybe more. My father rushes toward them.

"Is this real?" a deep voice asks in Urdu. "Are you all really standing before me now?" I look up to see Chacha Shahid, my father's brother, smiling at us. He looks as he does in all his pictures, large, with rounded shoulders and belly, his mustache black with flecks of gray. He pulls my father into a tight embrace. I only have a moment to watch them before I myself am engulfed in embraces.

My chachi stands dwarfed next to her husband, my chacha. Her face is pale; her cheeks are sallow. She wears a blue outfit and a matching blue nose ring. Their son, Sohail, born two months before Imran, now stands next to him, with hair that curls at the ears just like my own brother's. I see a smattering of small children, five at least, two girls in matching pink frocks and younger ones staring at all of us with mouths parted in awe. My father's sister, Phupo Hamida, wears a peach-colored outfit; her silver hair pokes through her scarf, her arms are crossed, her lips pressed together. My mother's sister, Khala Simki, leans in and kisses me with her bright pink lips; she has the same almond-shaped eyes and arched curve to her eyebrows as my mother. Except for her short hair, the reddish-brown color of rinsed henna, she looks like a younger version of my mother.

"Wow. I can't believe it. You're really here," says a girl's voice in Urdu. It's Selma, my cousin, smiling shyly in my direction. I recognize her instantly from the pictures our relatives send every year.

"Me either!" I respond. I'm thankful now for growing up speaking Urdu with my parents so that now I can effortlessly slip into the familiar language. "We've talked about coming forever, and now, just like that, here we are."

She tilts her head slightly. "I know people said we look alike, but it's almost like looking into a mirror."

I look back at her. I'm the oldest cousin in our family; at one year younger, Selma is second oldest. Her large eyes flanked by thick eyelashes, her height, her slender frame—

"We could be sisters," I tell her.

She laces her arm into mine and grins. "Well, we are already sisters."

"You must drive with us," a lanky man, my mother's brother, Mamu Latif, insists.

"Nonsense. They will ride with us," another says.

Protests break out in the parking lot. Each driver insists we ride with them.

"Enough." Chacha raises a thick hand. "They are staying with us. I will take them home." Everyone grows silent.

We squeeze into his blue car, and within minutes, we

rumble through the busy city of Lahore. The summer heat swelters, and beads of sweat trickle down my face as seven crammed bodies shift uncomfortably against one another, the air conditioner trying in vain to cool us all.

The streets are flooded with cars, some so old they cough out dark clouds of smoke with each forward motion. I see wiry men driving multicolored rickshaws, yellow cabs with black lettering, and cars moving as if traffic rules are optional. I look at the vendors on the side of the road pushing wooden carts, their clothes covered in soot as they call out their wares. Some tout fruits and vegetables. Others call out the prices of brown- and blond-haired dolls and bright yellow and pink plastic balls they push slowly down dusty roads.

As we drive along, the stores, with their huge lettering in English and Urdu announcing clothing and perfumes and seemingly stacked one atop the other, dwindle to a handful. And the road, although still bumpy and dusty, becomes considerably less crowded. The landscape slowly melts from the bustling city into the silence of country, with water buffalo and goats grazing while chickens perch on boundary walls or peck the ground.

"We're almost there," Chacha tells us. I glance over at Selma and smile. Getting to know family I've never met, exploring a part of the world I've never seen—suddenly spending a month in Pakistan doesn't feel daunting at all.

Chapter 10

My uncle's house resembles a fortress more than a home and is surrounded by a brick wall with a heavy steel gate. The flat roof makes the gray structure seem like a large concrete box. Many of the houses we passed seemed stuck against one another, much like townhomes. My uncle's home, in contrast, stands alone facing the dusty road that runs parallel to it.

The concrete walls inside are painted a fresh coat of white, but the gray floor lies stark under my feet in this foyer. My brother walks with Selma's brother, Sohail, down a corridor discussing video games and consoles.

"Want a tour?" Selma asks. I smile and nod.

"This is our drawing room, where we host guests." She points to the large room just off the foyer. Three white sofas flank three of the walls, and a large brilliant red rug with gold patchwork lends the otherwise simple room surprising warmth. Just off the drawing room is a large white dining table with matching white chairs and an imposing china cabinet behind it.

"This is the TV room," Selma says, pausing at the next room. She points to the large television taking up the better part of the far wall. Two brown couches are pressed together on the other side, and green rugs overlap one another, lining the floor.

"How many rooms are there?" I ask when we walk past another large living space just after the television room.

Selma laughs. "Well, this one we call our living room, because we do most of our living here."

That much is apparent already. Three of my younger cousins sit on the floor in this room whispering to one another while two others are playing carrom board and shrieking loudly with each flick of the game pieces. All four of the plush beige sofas in this room are filled with people, one of them my father. His brother, my chacha, sits to his left; his sister, my phupo, is to his right. Their hands are cupped, their heads lowered. I imagine they are making a silent prayer for their parents, who passed away. Between the shrieks of the children and laughter from other rooms that echo off the walls, it's difficult to focus on any conversation in particular.

I find my mother in the kitchen, standing next to the

stove. She smiles when she sees me. "Selma showing you around?" she asks. "You know, this isn't just any house. It has been in your father's family for almost one hundred years. He was born in this house. I lived here myself for a year when we got married."

"And who would have ever thought that this would be the next time you would return?" her sister, Khala Simki, says. Her eyes glisten with tears. "Twenty years. How did that happen?"

My mother moves to speak, but instead swallows. Her eyes grow moist.

"Now, now." Selma's mother, my chachi, puts a hand on my mother's shoulder. "No tears today. Just happiness. You have had a very long trip. Why don't you sit and relax while I finish making chai for everyone?"

"I can help," my mother insists. I watch her remove a wooden serving tray from one cabinet and teacups from another. She arranges the cups on the tray and then grabs a bowl of sugar from a drawer. How does she remember? I wonder. How is it that, after two decades away, it seems like she never left?

Selma and I continue the tour. We pass portraits of grim-faced family members encased in black frames hanging on the walls. She shows me all the bedrooms, until finally we are standing in front of hers.

"How many people live here?" I ask her.

"Well," she says, "our fathers' sister, Phupo Hamida, lives with us. She never got married, so where else can she go? Then there's the four of us: my parents, my brother, and me. We have space in the back room for Bilal, the servant. He's staying here while your family is here."

Bilal walks by us now. He is young and thin, and seems to nearly buckle under the weight of my suitcases.

Selma smiles. "You'll be sharing my room with me while you're here."

I step inside. Two beds lie on opposite ends; there's a small nightstand, a brown dresser, and an armoire on the far wall.

"I'm so glad your family is staying with us," she says. "Everyone wanted you to stay with them, but my father won. Not that there was ever any doubt. He always gets what he wants."

"Where does everyone else who is here live? There are at least thirty people."

"Most of our relatives seem like they live here, but they really don't," she says. "Almost all of them live in this village. Only your mother's family came from out of town. They'll stay with us too, while your family is here."

Khala Simki and her husband have five children. Her brother, Mamu Latif, and his wife have four. As though reading my mind, Selma laughs. "You just need a pillow and a blanket, and you can sleep anywhere really," she says.

"Still." I look around. Voices echo off the concrete walls outside. "We've really crowded you."

"It's fun," she insists. "School got out just yesterday. What's better than having your whole family all under one roof for the summer?"

As evening falls, everyone settles into the living room. A large pot of milky chai, along with an assortment of sweets, round and yellow, square and green, sits on the coffee table. Despite the sheer lack of space, more relatives, new ones I hadn't seen at the airport, continue to walk in, hugging me, pinching my cheeks, squeezing into empty spaces, and settling down.

"*No*. I saw you first." Mamu Latif waves a finger toward my mother. "You were dragging a suitcase—I saw you. You looked so confused!" he says.

"*Uff!*" my phupo scoffs at Latif. "I saw them first. I remember you all were scratching your heads wondering if you were at the wrong place when I saw them. Naila looked so bewildered. I thought her eyes would fall out!"

Everyone laughs, and I smile, taking a sip of the sweet, fragrant chai. The conversations around me slowly splinter off. In their photos, so many of my aunts and uncles posed somber-faced, but in person they are grinning, laughing, full to the brim with life.

"Want some tea too?" I ask Selma. She's sitting next to me.

"No, thanks. I don't really like tea," she says. Suddenly, her eyes brighten. "I forgot to show you my favorite part of the house. Do you want to go upstairs to see the rooftop?"

"The rooftop?"

"Yes, it's nice up there. Sometimes when the electricity goes out through the night, we even sleep up there." She gets up. "Come on, I'll show you."

I follow her to the kitchen and then I see where she's taking me, to the almost hidden stairs next to the fridge. We walk up the winding staircase, and then we're on the roof. I'm struck by the silence on the rooftop, its contrast to the laughter and noise downstairs. And the stars. They number more than I ever thought possible. For a moment, I am speechless.

"Since I was born, I've heard endless stories about your family," Selma says. "Nearly every day, our grand-mother used to say how much she wanted all of you to come back, at least just once."

"It was the same back home for us." I walk to the edge of the rooftop. "My parents always wanted to visit. It was all we ever heard growing up. How nice life is here and how much they wished we could see it."

"Nice?" Selma snorts. "Really? It's so boring and ordinary here. I always imagine what it must be like to live in the US. Sometimes I looked for hours at the pictures your family sent us, trying to imagine what it must be like in such an exciting place."

"No." I look out at the dusty street below, the mud-thatched homes in the distance. "This is different, but it's nice too."

"Just give it a few weeks," Selma assures me. "You will be so bored, you'll be dying to go back."

"We're only here for a month. I won't have a chance to get bored."

Chapter 11

The sound of children shrieking just outside our bedroom rouses me from sleep.

Selma, too, is getting up. She yawns and rubs her eyes. "Sorry. I can tell them to lower their voices."

"No, no. I'm up." My body aches from the long plane ride, but I'm too excited to go back to sleep.

The kitchen is full when I step inside. All the women are fluttering about at full speed, setting out plates, stirring pots on the stove, and rolling out dough.

"Almost done," my chachi announces. Large ceramic vessels of food are set on a long wooden table in the kitchen. Spiced chickpeas, sweet brown halva, ground keema with green peas, and a towering stack of buttered puris sit next to two large pitchers, one filled with sweet yogurt lassi and the other with salty-sweet lemonade.

All the tables and sofas are full, so I settle down on a spot on the rug just off the kitchen.

"Can I have a sip?" my five-year-old cousin Lubna asks me. The shyness from yesterday has all but evaporated. I nod and hand her my glass. "Thanks!" She grins and bounds off with it.

"Never trust Lubna," Selma says. She joins me on the ground. "Khala Simki doesn't like her having sweet things, so she takes it from others whenever she can."

Just then I see some children pass by outside, beyond the heavy metal gate. The sunlight shines over the dusty road, beckoning me.

"Could you show me around this village?" I ask her. "Sohail took Imran out yesterday, and I'd love to see what it's like too."

"Sure," she says. "But I'm not sure there is much to see."

"That's because you know it inside and out," I tease her. "And that's why I want you to give me the tour."

She laughs. "I can be an excellent tour guide. I better be. I've lived here all my life."

We step outside after breakfast, shielding our eyes from the sun with our hands. I trail behind Selma on the narrow path.

"This is the village market and where we get our fruit and vegetables. Meat is expensive, and they don't always have it, but it looks like they just got a fresh shipment." Selma points at a one-story open-air building with red carcasses hanging upside down at the entrance. "And if you like candy or biscuits, you go to Baba Toqeer. Sometimes he even makes pakoras and samosas." She gestures to a small store with a wooden counter.

"And over here—" Her words are interrupted just then by a high-pitched voice.

"Look who at long last finally arrived!" A spindly woman in a white chador steps out of her house.

"Rubina," Selma whispers in my ear. "She's a gossip, so just be careful what you say."

"Imtiaz's girl?" she asks. She steps up close to me and squints. "Yes, it sure is. Look at those eyes. I'd know them anywhere. You look like your father's side of the family, don't you?"

"I guess so." I tuck a strand of hair behind my ear and glance at Selma.

"Imtiaz's daughter?" Another person now approaches us. A man. He wears a brown salwar kamiz. Next to him stands a woman with a gold nose ring, balancing a baby on her hip.

"It's Naila, right?" the woman with the nose ring asks. I nod, and she smiles.

"How are you?" Selma asks. "Naila, this is Haris bhai and his wife, Sadeya baji. They're our next-door neighbors. I was just showing Naila around the village."

"I have to admit I didn't really believe you were coming when people started saying it again," Haris bhai says. He glances at his wife. "It's just we've been hearing your family is coming every year since you were born. And now how old are you?"

"Seventeen," I reply.

"So we've been waiting seventeen years," he says.

"You like it here so far?" Rubina asks. "Feel like home? This is your home, you know. If your family hadn't just run off, you'd be from here, just like us."

I stare at her, unsure how to respond to what sounds like an accusation.

"Oh"—she laughs—"don't make that face! I'm only joking. I'm your phupo's oldest friend. She's like my sister, really. She'll tell you herself not to mind me."

Selma tugs my elbow and smiles at them. "We have to get going. I promised my mom we'd be home soon."

"Nice to meet you," I tell them.

"Sorry," Selma says as we continue on. "We don't get a lot of people from out of town."

We pass a group of children playing cricket in a grassy field to our left. They are shouting and laughing until they see us. Then they stop, their bats lowered, and look over at us.

"Those children"—she nods to them—"they're Seema's. She lives three houses down from us."

"All ten?" I count again.

I wave to the children. A small chubby girl with a red frock takes a step forward, but an older sibling puts a hand on her shoulder to stop her.

I flash my biggest smile and then they smile back at me; the youngest girl waves as we pass.

We walk past a few nondescript concrete buildings. The front door of one of them is propped open by a metal chair. "We get our clothes stitched here," Selma tells me. "We don't buy any fabric from him because the quality of his fabric is poor, but we are lucky to have him in our village, because he stitches very well. He's going to stitch your clothing too."

Just then, a melodic sound echoes through the air. I recognize it instantly—it's the call to prayer.

"The masjid is on the other side of our house, but the loudspeakers help us hear it wherever we are," Selma says. "My father usually goes, but I can take you there sometime."

I listen to the familiar words I've grown up hearing and smile at the beautiful, lyrical sounds that make me suddenly feel like I am home.

It takes less than ten minutes from there to make it to the last store. A few more people stop to greet us. Some wave from where they sit in front of their homes. I'm aware of others too, eyes peering at us from the windows of homes we pass. It's a strange feeling to be so interesting to so many people.

Four large trees with thick green leaves surround the last store, and then there is nothing beyond it but an endless expanse of fields.

"This road connects us to other villages. But I've never walked farther than this point right here." Selma looks down at her pink sandals.

I want to ask her why, but something in the way she says it stops me.

As we make our way back to the house, we pass a large stretch of grassy land.

"These are our family's sugarcane and orange groves," Selma says, following my gaze.

Thick green stalks gently sway side to side and sparse pockets of orange dot green trees in the fields in the distance.

"It's so shaded. Can we go there?"

We step through the curtain of sugarcane stalks. They are thick, some so tall they tower over us. The dirt is softer here. My feet sink into it. We walk until we are in the orange groves. I look around. We are enveloped in a canopy of trees filled with lush green leaves.

"It's cooler here," I tell her. "Not as hot as when we were out on the road."

"The canes are juicy in the winter, and the oranges

grow so sweet, they taste like sugar. The shade is always nice here. We played here a lot as kids, but it's been a long time since I've been back."

Later that afternoon, standing on the roof, I take in the roads I walked with Selma, the expanse of my family's fields, and in the distance, what seem like brick and clay makings of other homes in other villages farther away, perhaps much like the one I now gaze from.

I watch my father in the evening. He hums to himself, a book under his arm. He walks to the kitchen and grabs a cup of tea, on his way to the rooftop. My mother sits, as she has since this morning, with Khala Simki. I haven't seen them pause even once in their endless stream of conversation.

I watch my mother now as she whispers in Khala Simki's ear. Suddenly, they both lean away, and their peals of laughter echo off the walls.

I try to remember if I've ever seen my mother like this. So carefree and lighthearted.

I can't.

I see now why she wanted to come here. Florida might be where she lives. But Pakistan is home.

The red phone Saif gave me stays nestled deep inside my satchel. We've texted, but I have yet to speak to him. I miss his voice. His touch. But I'll talk to him soon.

For the first time in a long time, I feel hopeful.

Chapter 12

I follow Selma down the dirt path that connects our home to my chacha's orange fields. It's where Selma and I spend most of our afternoons now. The days are flying by faster than I could have imagined. I can't believe how long we've been here. I love sitting here hidden in the orange groves, just me and Selma, drinking soda and exchanging stories about our lives.

Every story, except the one I most want to share.

I sit down on a grassy patch and tilt my head back, finishing the last of the soda.

"You know I'm just happy to spend time with you, but I don't know why you like to do this, sitting out here when it's so hot." Selma lifts an arm and shades her eyes from the sun poking through the leaves.

"The sun starts to feel nice after a little bit. Kind of a toasty feeling."

"Maybe, if you're a roti on the stove." She scrutinizes

me for a moment. "Are you maybe part roti, Naila? That would explain everything."

"Oh, stop." I laugh and swat her shoulder. "It's hot in Florida too. I guess I'm just used to it."

"Well, it's nice to be away from all the noise in the house." She leans back, her elbows propping her up. "And to talk without getting constantly interrupted by twenty little ones."

I cross my legs and look at her. "Speaking of talking," I say, "we've talked about everything under the sun except what every girl talks about the most. You now know all about the food I like, the way I decorated my bedroom, and what I wear to school, but we've never talked about other stuff."

"What other stuff?" She tilts her head toward me.

"Boys. Do you like anyone?"

At this Selma straightens up; her smile vanishes. "No. I don't like anyone."

"I'm sorry," I rush. "It's just, you know, you're like a sister to me, and, well, back home, girls talk about things like that."

She studies her hands but says nothing.

I open my mouth to apologize again. We've had such an easy rapport, but I can tell by the way she looks away that I've made her uncomfortable.

"I'm sorry." She studies the leaves in the distance for a moment before looking at me. She gives me a tentative smile. "It's just my parents. If they ever heard me talking about something like that, they'd be so angry . . ." Her voice trails off.

"No, it's okay," I assure her. "I shouldn't have said anything."

That evening, I step into the bedroom and close the door. Reaching into my purse, I take out my cell phone. I sift through the texts from just this morning.

Let's talk tonight, your time.

I'll try.

I'll be waiting.

My fingers rest on the digits. I'm tempted to dial his number. Just to hear him on the other end, even if I cannot speak.

I hear my small cousins run past the bedroom door, their bare feet smacking against the tiles. Their voices are loud, and their laughter echoes off the walls.

I can't.

I can't take the risk.

I hold down the red button until the screen goes black.

Chapter 13

Naila." There's a knock on the door.

Selma and I look up with a start. We're lying on her twin bed, a stack of magazines between us. Some are mine from the plane ride, but most are Pakistani magazines that belong to Selma. We're leafing through Selma's right now, inspecting and picking out our favorites among the array of high-end saris, lenghas, and the latest salwar kamizes.

My mother opens the door and steps inside. "What are you both doing holed up in here?"

"Sorry." I look at the clock on the wall. "I didn't realize it was almost lunchtime. Do you need help?"

"We have some guests coming over for chai in a little over an hour. You need to get ready."

"Who?" I ask.

"Family friends." My mother walks up to the armoire and rifles through the hanging clothes. "You'd think with how much we're paying him, the tailor would have gotten your clothes done by now," she murmurs. "Selma, you don't mind if Naila wears one of your outfits again, do you?" Without waiting for an answer, she pulls out a lavender silk salwar kamiz. "Thank God you and Selma are the same size. This will do."

"That? Kind of fancy, isn't it?"

"We're guests, Naila." My mother looks at me. "We dress up when people come over. Now, hurry up and iron this, and then I need your help with the chai."

I watch her go. Her words leave me subdued. They remind me that while she may be happier here, she is still not happy with me.

"What are you going to wear?" I ask Selma.

She shrugs. "They're not coming to see me."

"Want me to pick out an outfit for you?"

"I'm just going to stay in the kitchen."

"They're not my friends," I tell her. "You have to sit with me. Who else am I going to talk to?"

I wait for her to say something more. Instead, to my surprise, she gets up and walks out.

I iron the clothes and brush my hair. When I hear the knock on the door, I step into the hallway.

"Good." My chachi approaches me. "Just in time. Selma's in the kitchen. Help her with the chai."

"Sure." I walk toward the front door.

"Where are you going?" she asks.

"To greet the guests."

"No"—she shakes her head—"we need you to help with the tea first."

"They're my parents' friends. They'll be offended if I don't greet them."

"They'll be offended if the chai is not ready in time. Please, Naila."

Her mouth is pressed into a smile, but I see the apprehension in her eyes.

"Okay," I finally say.

I walk into the kitchen. Selma is standing over the stove drizzling a stream of milk into a boiling dark vat of steeped tea. Khala Simki opens and shuts cupboards, finally pulling out a silver tin of biscuits.

"So is this a 'world's fastest tea' competition?" I ask Selma.

Selma laughs at this and whispers, "Quiet. You know they can hear us. These walls don't hold secrets."

"But seriously"—I lower my voice—"the doorbell rang two minutes ago, and we're working like they're starving in the other room."

"Can you help arrange the tray, Naila?" Khala Simki shoots me a look.

I look back at Selma, but she is now focused on the task at hand. The laughter has vanished.

"Good." Khala Simki nods when she sees the teacups I've arranged. Selma pours the tea into a ceramic teapot and rests it in the center of the wooden tray. "Now take this out and go meet the guests."

I stare at the tray. "Selma would be better at it. I've never done it before."

"Nonsense." Khala Simki smiles. "Why do they want to see Selma? They can see her anytime."

I look up at Selma. The remark lands like the slap I thought it was. Her cheeks grow crimson.

Before I can respond, Khala Simki ushers me on. "Go now."

I pick up the tray and try to keep it steady. The teacups clink together loudly. I make my way down the hallway into the drawing room, where the guests are seated. The room is filled with subdued chatter that ceases once I enter.

I place the tray on the coffee table. An older woman with an elaborate peacock pendant sits next to two younger women. One, her hair cut in a severe bob, is looking down at her feet; the other woman cradles a little girl in her arms. The other two men, I imagine their husbands, sit across from them. The younger one with curly brown hair smiles at me. He reminds me a little of Imran. I smile back at him and move to greet them when my mother interrupts me.

"Naila," she says. I turn to her. She motions to the empty seat next to her. I walk over and sit down.

I look out toward the hallway to see who else will join us, but no one does.

"Well, that was weird," I tell my mother after the guests leave. "They barely talked the whole time we were there."

"You shouldn't call people weird," my mother says. "You're in a different place, and things are done differently here."

"But still," I insist. "That was strange."

"It was nice of them to come," she says. She looks at my outfit. "We are going to a dinner tonight. You should change out of this so it doesn't get dirty before we go. And be careful because if the tailor isn't done with your clothes, you may have to wear it to the lunch we're going to tomorrow as well."

"Wow." I stare at her. "That's a lot of parties."

"We're not here for long, so everybody wants to host us. We can't refuse."

"So it will be dinners and teas for the rest of the week until we leave?"

"Well, actually," she says, "your father looked into it, and we can extend our trip for an extra week."

"We're not going back on Wednesday?"

"It was last-minute, but it's nice, isn't it? Aren't you having a good time here? After twenty years, one month just started feeling too short."

One extra week might actually be nice. I'll still get back to school in time for my orientation.

But I do need to figure out how to tell Saif.

Chapter 14

The next afternoon, I step into the courtyard with Selma and Imran. The electricity is out again. These blackouts come and go without warning, but today the breeze outside helps ease the discomfort. Phupo is sitting alone. She's holding a felt pipe connected to an odd-looking cylindrical pot resting on a low-seated stool next to her. Her silver hair, uncovered today, is wrapped in a loose braid.

"What's that?" Imran asks.

She looks up at us, startled. "I didn't see you all there." She pauses for a moment. "It's a hookah," she finally says. I watch her inhale from the pipe and blow out a plume of smoke.

"Can I try?" Imran asks. "Or is it too complicated?"

"If you know how to breathe, you know how to use a hookah," Selma says.

"Come on over and try it," Phupo tells him.

Imran sits down next to her.

"Imran," I tell him, "if our parents catch us doing this, you're going to be dead."

At this Phupo scoffs. "Your father is the one who taught me how to smoke it. Let him try to get mad." She takes a puff and exhales, sending a large circle of smoke spiraling into the air. I watch my brother eagerly take the pipe. He takes a puff—and then falls to his side, overcome by a fit of coughing.

"Don't feel bad!" Selma says. "That happened to me too the first and last time I tried it."

"I bet I can do it." Sitting next to Imran, I take the pipe from him. I take a puff and release a faint stream of gray smoke. "Look! I'm a natural!" I take another puff, and then——my throat burns, my eyes water, and I lean forward, coughing.

"Take it easy." Phupo starts laughing, and soon we're all laughing, unable to stop, tears streaming down our faces.

"Well, at least I have a cool story about my cool aunt to tell when I go back home," I say when I recover. I look at the hookah pipe in my hands and turn to my aunt. "Phupo, did my father really smoke this?"

"This very one," she says. "We spent countless nights, all of us, watching the stars above, smoking hookah, and talking about the dreams we had for our lives."

"I know he wanted to be a doctor," I tell her. "That's why he's so supportive of me."

She looks at me, but I notice her smile falters. Does talking about my father's unfulfilled dreams remind her of her own unfulfilled hopes? I'm sure she hadn't dreamed of living here with her younger brother and no family of her own. She says nothing for a moment.

"Your parents are too hard on you," she finally says. "You're a good kid."

For a minute, I don't understand, and then my face flushes. Did my father confide in her his disappointment in me?

"That thing is lethal," Imran interrupts. "But I want to try it again. Practice makes perfect."

He is reaching for the hookah pipe in my hand when we hear my mother's voice.

"Naila!"

I turn around. My mother and Khala Simki approach us. "What on earth do you think you're doing, Naila?" my mother says. "I have been looking all over for you, and this is where you are? Smoking hookah?"

"Mehnaz," Phupo interrupts, "we're just having a little fun, that's all."

"Yeah," Imran says. "If you're going to get mad at her, you have to get mad at me too. I was doing it first."

My mother steps closer to me. "Now you smell like

smoke." She sighs. "Let's go get ready. We're running late."

"Again?" I ask. "That's the second time today."

"How about Naila stays back just this once?" Imran asks. "It's not like they're going to miss her. They want to see you guys."

Selma looks at my disappointed expression and chimes in. "Baba Toqeer has fresh pakoras today. We were talking about going to get some. Maybe just this once?"

"What a thing to say!" Khala Simki exclaims. "You all can get pakoras together anytime. I'll make you some tomorrow."

We hear the whirring sound of a fan coming back to life.

"Perfect." Khala Simki turns to look at the house. "The lights are back on. Now, go get ready. I already have your outfit hanging in your room."

I want to push a little more and point out how Imran is yet again not required to go. How he's been to only a few of these gatherings. But I bite my lip. I know that's an argument I won't win. It's an argument that predates my time here.

Chapter 15

I step into the bedroom and press my back against the door. Reaching into my purse, I take out my cell phone. Since arriving, I still have only been able to text Saif. But I need to talk to him. A text will not suffice to tell him about the delay.

Just then, there is a knock. I quickly stuff the phone back into my purse and open the door.

"Sorry," Selma says. "Your khala wants me to get ready too."

"My parents have a lot of friends." I shake my head. "A lot of boring friends."

"What can you do?" she responds.

My mother smiles at me when I step outside. Her frustration from moments ago seems to have vanished. I wonder how much of her smile is her slowly forgiving me and how much is her not wanting everyone to know how unhappy with me she remains.

"Do you think maybe we could go sightseeing one day?" I ask her. "We go to so many dinners and teas, but maybe it would be nice to see a little more of Pakistan." I adjust the maroon bangles on my arms. "We hardly eat a meal at home anymore."

"We'll go soon," my mother says. "It's just been so long since we've been back. Everyone wants to see us or have us over. We can't refuse them."

"Is this what you're wearing?" Khala Simki walks up to me. "Didn't you see the outfit I had hanging for you? Never mind—I know an even better one."

"What's wrong with this one?" I run my hands over my maroon georgette salwar kamiz. "Ami thought it looked nice."

"Naila." Khala Simki clucks her tongue. "It is nice, but the tailor just finished making you so many beautiful clothes. There's no need to wear these outdated ones from Selma's closet."

"But it's nice," I protest.

Khala Simki takes my hand and leads me toward the bedroom. "It's fine for being at home, but at the home of someone who is not family, you must be a bit more careful."

She sifts through the white plastic bags of clothing fresh from the family tailor. "Here!" she pulls out a yellow salwar kamiz with gold embroidery on the cuffs. "It doesn't even need ironing!" Her eyes glance over my purse. "If you wanted to leave that thing behind just this once, I'm sure no one will steal it."

"I know. I'd just rather take it with me." I watch her leave. My purse is large and orange with big black flowers. I can fit everything I need to inside it, most importantly the cell phone hidden deep within. That aspect of my wardrobe, they have now learned, is nonnegotiable.

"Remember," Khala Simki says in the car that afternoon, "we don't talk too loudly or too much. You can do enough of that at home." She casts a sharp look at Selma. Selma's smile fades before she looks out the window.

We step into a modest home much like the townhomes we saw dotting the landscape when we first arrived.

I watch the men walk toward the back door. My father's friend opens the door and leads them onto the verandah.

"Please come sit," the hostess, a petite woman with a crooked nose in a purple salwar kamiz and matching headscarf, tells us, ushering us into the drawing room.

The hostess carries in a tray of glasses filled with ice and Coca-Cola. I take one and look at my mother. She's holding a glass in her hands. My aunts talk quietly among themselves.

We just arrived, I think. *Already it feels endless.*

"Can you cook rice?" the hostess asks.

I look at her for a second. A spoonful of rice hovers over my plate. "What? Oh, uh, yes, I can cook rice."

"Boiled, or with tarka?" She scratches her ear.

I glance at my mother. What kind of crazy friends are these? I hear my father's voice in the distance, the sound of faint laughter. My aunts wear strained expressions, waiting for my response. The hostess looks at me with an equally expectant expression.

"I can make both," I finally tell her.

The hostess breaks into a large smile. "What a surprise! Your mother raised you well."

That afternoon I climb into the car, squeezing in next to Selma. "What was that about?" I mutter. "Why don't they ask you any questions?"

Selma shrugs. "You're the one from America. I guess I'm not as interesting as you."

I stare at her. She frowns and twists her dupatta with her fingers. I've noticed that anytime we go to a party, she sulks and our comfortable rapport completely vanishes. And then it hits me. All the questions about my life back home, the food I eat, the clothes I wear, and now, all the attention doted on me, everyone wanting to talk to me. The hosts at these parties act as if Selma is not even in the room. Selma has been my dearest friend since I've come to Pakistan, but—

She's jealous, I realize.

I look at the back of her head while she gazes out the car window. Maybe I'd feel the same if the situation were reversed. It can't be easy for her to see everyone giving me so much attention. I want to give her a hug and tell her she has nothing to feel jealous about. That she has no idea how annoying it is to be gawked at like a roadside carnival exhibit just because you're not from around here.

But will that really change her feelings? I lean back into my seat. We won't be here much longer. Only a few more days until it's time to go home. Then Selma can go back to the life she had.

Chapter 16

$\mathcal{I}$'m hoping to have a moment alone when we get back home to call Saif. But as usual, I'm interrupted by the sound of small footsteps and then knocks pounding on the bedroom door. I open it. Maaria, my youngest cousin, lifts her plump arms up. I suppress a frustrated sigh.

I can't wait much longer. I need to talk to Saif. Today.

I lift Maaria up and make my way to the kitchen. All the women are here. Selma is sitting on a stool, laughing at a conversation between my mother and aunts. Ami's eyes brighten when she sees me. Selma slides to the edge of her stool, making room for me.

"Come over. We're settling an important matter."

"What's that?" Maaria squirms and slides out of my arms.

"Ami says chai isn't chai if you don't add cinnamon, and your khala thinks—"

"That if you add too many flavors, it becomes its

own meal, totally defeating the purpose," Khala Simki finishes.

I sit pressed next to Selma and listen to their conversation, jumping as it always does from one topic to the next. The fan circles overhead at a steady hum.

Just then, I hear footsteps. My father. He walks up to the counter. "Chai? If you are making some, I will not decline a cup."

"Of course!" Khala Simki exclaims. "We are making it for you, after all."

I am watching him go up the stairs, teacup in hand, when suddenly it hits me: the rooftop.

Of course.

Suddenly I feel lighter as I think of Saif.

I pull the bedsheet to my chest and strain my ears. Silence. I squint at the glowing display of my phone: 4:00 A.M.

I sit up and slip on my sandals. I look over at Selma, but her eyes are shut, her breathing steady. I turn the knob to the door and open it just wide enough to slip outside.

My eyes slowly adjust to the pitch-black hallway. I press my hands against the concrete wall, feeling my way to the entrance of the stairs, and make my way up, praying it's unoccupied tonight. Mamu Latif and his family already left, and Khala Simki's husband has also gone home. The house is emptier, and I breathe a sigh of relief—the flat space is empty. The air is thin and cool. I walk to the edge of the rooftop. I am engulfed in darkness, invisible. I pull out my phone and dial the number. The phone rings, and my stomach fills with butterflies for both the chance to finally talk to him and for what I have to say.

"Hello?" His voice sounds crisp, clearer than I expected.

"Saif! I can't believe it's you!"

"Naila. Are you okay?"

"Of course I'm okay. Why wouldn't I be?"

"I don't know." He exhales. "I just haven't talked to you in so long! I miss you."

"I'm fine. Really. The rooms in the house echo, and there are so many of us staying here that it's impossible to find a minute alone. If it wasn't for this rooftop, I'm not sure we'd be able to talk at all."

"It's okay. It's just, finally, I get to hear your voice. I'm counting down the days until Wednesday. I think Carla is too, the way she's blowing up my phone every day asking if you're back yet. I can't wait to see you. I can come out to the same spot we met at last time?"

"Well . . ." My voice trails off.

"It's Wednesday, right?"

"No, you're right." I pace the rooftop. "Well, you *were* right. We were supposed to come back that day. It's just that the trip got extended a little bit."

"What do you mean?"

"My parents extended our trip an extra week, but don't worry, it's fine. I'm actually having a good time here."

He's quiet for a minute.

"It's okay, Saif, really. You should see my parents. They're laughing and smiling. It's almost like nothing happened. I think this trip is going to help them relax, help them see things better when we get back, about us. Orientation isn't until mid-July anyways. Honestly, the longer we're here, the happier they look."

"That's great," he finally says. "I just miss you, I guess."

"I know. I miss you too. But it's just an extra week. I'll see you soon."

We hang up the phone, and I smile and press it close to me.

Chapter 17

I pull my suitcase to the ground. The week is nearly over. Time passed faster than I could have imagined with my days spent with Selma, wandering the house, the village, and sharing stories. Imran, Sohail, Selma, and I even managed to make our way over to the watering hole bordering the village, where my father once learned to swim. We promised not to splash one another but came home dripping with water, laughing so hard, our stomachs ached.

I unzip my suitcase now and fold my clothes, gather my books, and collect the white plastic bags holding newly stitched clothing, some I have yet to even try on. I set the suitcase against the bedroom wall before heading toward the kitchen.

Passing by the bedroom where my parents are staying, I glance inside.

This can't be right.

I look at the quilted bedspread, the lacy pillows propped up against the wall, and the large black suitcases with pink stitching on the handles. They lie open and empty, side by side in the corner of the room, just as they have since we arrived. I step inside and walk to the closet. My mother's clothes are still on their metal hangers. On my father's nightstand, his books of poetry are still stacked like a leaning tower.

I make my way to Imran's room. He's lying on the bed with his eyes closed, tapping his foot. One headphone is in his ear, while my cousin Sohail listens with the other. Sohail's eyes are closed, his arms limp and to his side; small snores escape his mouth.

"Imran?" I knock on the open door. Imran gives me a half wave. I walk into the room, stepping over his newly purchased CDs scattered across the floor. "Why aren't you packed?"

Imran removes the white earpiece from his ear and sits up. "Why would I be packed?"

"Because we're leaving tomorrow."

"Tomorrow? You mean Ami didn't tell you? They extended our ticket again. We're staying at least another month."

Blood rushes to my head. A week was fine, but a month? And from what Imran just said, an uncertain month at that, tempered with the words *at least*?

"What's wrong?" Imran asks. "You look like you're going to throw up."

"It's just . . . my college orientation. It's next week. I already told Carla I'd room with her." But the thought that sticks hardest: *Why am I the last to know?*

"That sucks," Imran says. "They must have just forgotten with us being here and everything. Just tell them, they can always change their plans."

"Aren't you upset about it? Don't you want to go home too?"

"Nah. Abu bought Sohail a PlayStation and I can buy all the bootleg DVDs I want. I'm cool with staying."

"One month!" Saif exclaims into the phone. It's four o'clock in the morning. His loud voice makes me wince. "This is insane! What about orientation?"

"I know." I grip the phone tightly. "I'm angry too. I went to talk to them after my brother told me, but they just kind of brushed it off. I didn't want to make a scene in front of everyone. There are just always so many people here. So many interruptions," I tell him. "Don't worry, I'm going to talk to them tomorrow and figure out what's going on."

"You're going to miss the tour. The sign-up for mentoring. The mixers. Everything. Why are they doing this?"

"They probably forgot about orientation," I tell him. "When I talk to them in the morning, I'm sure it'll all get straightened out. Maybe I can leave earlier." I hope desperately that what I'm saying is true. What I don't tell him is just how unnerving those unpacked suitcases in my parents' bedroom really were.

The next morning, I find my mother in the kitchen with my aunts, mixing spicy potatoes into dough for breakfast. She slathers butter onto the flattened bread before she hands it to my aunt to toss onto the stove. Chachi stands by the stove, pouring milk into a large metal pot for our tea.

We should be on a plane right now, I think. *We should be halfway around the world.* And yet here my mother stands, as though nothing is the matter. She laughs, lost in conversation, so busy she doesn't notice me standing there. I don't know how to get her alone to begin the conversation I know I must have.

After breakfast, I find my opportunity when my mother walks unaccompanied out into the courtyard. I make my way outside. She sits on a bench underneath a thin drooping tree, a glass of water in one hand.

I sit next to her. "I thought we were leaving by now. I've packed and everything." I force a laugh. "When is the flight? When are we leaving?"

"Hmm, the flight?" She takes a sip of water and looks at me.

"Ami, Imran told me we might be here for a month longer. That's not true, is it?"

My mother waves a hand to swat a fly buzzing close to her face. "No. We were considering a month, but your father and I were talking yesterday, and we changed our minds." She takes another sip of water.

I let out a deep breath. A simple misunderstanding, that's all this was.

"The biggest issue was the dry cleaning business," she continues. "Ever since your father opened the second one, it's been so busy, but luckily, Javier needs more hours. He told your father he's handling both fine, so we're going to stay for the rest of the summer."

No. I stare at her. *This can't be happening.* "But, Ami, my college orientation! It's next week."

"Naila, really! Your orientation? How often do we come to Pakistan? Do you have any idea how much these tickets cost your father? This trip is not all about you. You can orient yourself when you get back."

"But it's mandatory." My voice trembles. "Abu already paid for it."

"Call them and let them know. I'm sure they'll understand."

But I don't understand. I don't understand any of this. I watch her, but her lips are pressed together, her eyes no longer meeting mine. Words form but refuse to take shape. *My father,* I think. *If I have any hope of reasoning with someone, it will be with him.*

Chapter 18

I walk into the kitchen the next morning. My mother, Khala Simki, and Chachi are huddled over the stove.

"They said it was one hundred acres of land, but you can safely say it's no more than fifty-five."

"Yes, but that is easy enough to check, isn't it? Maybe we could call around and ask."

"Ami?"

All three faces swivel to face me.

"Naila, what is it?" my mother asks.

"I was wondering where Abu was."

"Your father? He's on the rooftop, where else?"

I run through my talking points with each step, revising my arguments, making them clearer in my mind. *The money is already paid. I don't want to fall behind on everything before I even begin college. If I don't go, I'll have to spend time when I should be studying to figure out my way around.*

My father is reading a newspaper on the light brown

woven charpoy on the rooftop. His glasses tilt slightly down the bridge of his nose.

"Abu?"

He looks up at me. "This is the first time I've seen you on your own without your twin, Selma, at your side."

"She's asleep. I came here to talk to you about something, actually." I sit down next to him on the charpay and flash him my biggest smile, trying my best to mask my nerves.

"Sure. What's the matter?"

I shift in my seat. "First, I want to thank you and Ami for this trip. Even though it's been a little hot, I'm having a great time."

"It's been very hot—that's why we haven't gone sightseeing yet. But now that we're staying longer, we can make some plans and explore a bit."

"Abu, as much as I love being here, my college orientation is next week, remember? The university said attendance was mandatory. If I don't do the orientation now, I'll be behind when I get there to start classes."

"I know." My father wipes his glasses with his kamiz. "Your mother told me. I'm going to call the university and see if they can give you a waiver. I'm sure it won't be a problem. You can also use one of our calling cards to call Carla and—"

"No, that's not what I want," I interrupt. "I'm going to fall behind before I even start."

My father frowns, but I plunge forward. "I know how happy you are here, but you don't have to cut your trip short for me. I could go back early. I'll be living on my own soon anyways."

Just then I hear footsteps. My mother emerges from the stairwell.

"We just made the best parathas!" Her smile fades. "What's wrong?" She places a hand on my shoulder, giving it a squeeze.

"Just talking to your daughter. She has an interesting proposition."

"Oh?" she asks. She looks down at me.

"Yes." My father removes his glasses and folds them. I watch him place them in his pocket. "She had the brilliant idea"—he laughs—"that she could just go back home without us. She was wondering if that would be okay."

"Naila." My mother's hand falls from my shoulder. "Drop it."

She looks at my father. He looks at her.

No one speaks.

Finally, my father stands up. "Let's go. We don't want to keep everyone waiting."

I watch them walk away from me. I watch them disappear down the stairwell. Neither of them even turns to see if I'm following.

Neither seems to care that I have not moved from where I am sitting.

But this is not what disturbs me.

I understand their refusal. I know they have yet to forgive me. But what was that look? The brief look my parents exchanged? I've known them my whole life. I know their glances, their smiles, their frowns, but this? This was a look completely unfamiliar.

Chapter 19

I wander into my room and sit down on the bed. I look at my luggage resting against the wall. How many times have I packed and unpacked these belongings? I yank the luggage and shove it into the closet.

It's been one week since I spoke to my parents. I'm trying my best to accept this. I throw myself into the rhythm as best I can, but it's difficult. Most of our relatives left long ago, but Khala Simki stays, and the house rings with her laughter.

Each day is beginning to blend into the next. I don't get up early anymore. I close my eyes when my young cousins totter in, and I pretend to be asleep. The blinding heat that once felt like a minor annoyance now stifles me. I miss my bed. Hot water that doesn't suddenly turn icy cold. I miss coffee and chocolate cake and—*I miss Saif.* I miss him so much, it physically hurts.

I wrap a light chador around myself and walk to the

window. The fan overhead casts a cool breeze. Dark gray clouds hang heavy in the sky, moving slowly in my direction. The phone vibrates against me. It's Saif. He's called three times today. A fat raindrop splashes onto the windowsill. I reach inside my purse, feeling for the phone. Just then, there's a knock at the door.

Khala Simki steps inside and peers through the unlit room. "Why are you in the dark?" She turns on the lamp near my bed and joins me by the window. "Good. We needed rain. Maybe it will clear the dust outside." She puts her arm around me. "Always lost in your thoughts." She smiles at me. Then, her eyes light up. "Oh! Look at me, forgetting why I'm even here. Sumbul—you met her at a lunch party last week, remember?—she's coming in a few minutes. Help me get some things together."

I press my hands on the windowsill. The door clicks shut behind me. I don't remember Sumbul. And I don't care. I've met so many people, they're blending into one blurred image. I bite my lip. Half the summer to go and more dinner parties and tea times than I can possibly imagine. I shudder.

I am pulling out a blue outfit from the armoire when I hear my brother's voice in the hallway.

"One hundred rupees, Ami, please."

"Take some more and share it with your cousins, okay?

Don't let them pay for anything when you go out with them."

"We're just going to the watering hole."

"Well, stop and get some sweets or samosas if there are any. Your cousins would like that, and if you remember, bring some back for the house."

I draw in a sharp intake of breath. I want to go with Imran and Sohail. I want the welcome relief the water lends from the sticky heat that clings to everyone. Even if I couldn't wade in, just to sit in the light drizzle of this rain would be enough today. I consider asking my mother, but I already know the answer.

"Are you okay?" Selma says. We're standing in the kitchen. She is helping me lay out sweets on a copper tray and fill the sugar pot. "You don't seem like yourself lately."

"I'm fine." I keep my eyes fixed on the hot liquid pouring out of the spout.

"Maybe we could go out today, after it stops raining. It's been a while since we've done that."

"Yeah, maybe. Maybe if I could get a chance to breathe for a second too. Maybe if these guests ever stopped coming."

Selma looks up at me with a start.

"I'm sorry. I didn't mean to say it like that." I lean over and hug her. "I'm just so tired of it. I mean, it's nice, everyone is so friendly, but it's annoying to always have to entertain people."

"The chai is almost out," my khala calls out from the drawing room in a singsong voice loud enough for me to hear.

I step into the drawing room and find a smaller group this time. I set the tray down on the coffee table.

"Naila, come join us," my mother says. I look up for Selma, but she has disappeared behind the kitchen door.

"We were just talking about you," the female visitor says as I sit down next to my mother on the corner couch. She's wearing a pink outfit with pearl earrings. I look at the others. Her husband, round in shape with a long graying beard, sits next to my father. "How are you liking it here in Pakistan?" the woman asks.

"I like it," I respond.

"It's wonderful you speak Urdu so well. Your parents did a good job. Do you know how to sew and stitch as well?"

I stare at her. I've been asked many strange questions, but this is the first time anyone has asked me this.

"Naila," my mother finally says, "go check on Selma. See what she's up to."

I'm so sick of these gatherings. I want my own life back. Hot tears threaten to emerge. I walk past the TV room. My girl cousins, even Selma, are watching television. I glance outside.

The rain has stopped.

I don't think. I don't let myself second-guess. I need to get out of here. Gripping my purse, I unlatch the front door and slip outside, shutting it quietly behind me. A gentle mist envelops me as I make my way down the road, trying my best to stay on the small patches of grass, avoiding the puddles filling potholes in the street.

A group of children are playing cricket on the grassy field across the street. Cries of cheating and arguments drift through the air toward me. Except for them, the damp roads are empty. I walk past the small stores selling sweets and groceries until I reach the last store on the street. I glance around, but the street remains empty. I slip behind the store and press open my phone, dialing his number. I will tell him everything. I need a comforting voice, someone who will just tell me everything will be okay.

"This is ridiculous!" His loud voice hurts my ears. "Are you going to let them just tell you what to do?"

"What do you want me to say to them? I've tried everything—they're not listening!"

"You have to keep trying! You can't take no for an answer."

"If I could do something, I would. You know I've been trying. I just don't know what else to do. I feel so power-less." Tears flood my face.

"Wait, Naila, no, I'm sorry. I don't mean to yell at you. I'm not mad at you. I'm sorry. I'm just frustrated. I'm worried." He pauses. "I love you."

I make my way back to the house, fighting back tears. I've done my best to be positive, to make the best of this situation, but I can't push away the heavy feeling pressing down on me like I'm suffocating. I unlatch the metal gate to my uncle's home. I try my best to appear calm and unaffected, but my chest feels as if it might burst from pain.

I'm so far away from Saif.

I stare up at this house. It's my father's home too. It's my home, they tell me. But right now, all I can see is a large cinder box that traps me inside.

Chapter 20

No one seems to have noticed my absence. My cousins are still watching television. The guests have left, and my mother is in deep conversation with my aunts. I head to the bedroom I share with Selma.

I need to be alone.

The curtains are drawn over the windows. The room is pitch-dark. Pressing my purse close to me, I drop to the floor at the foot of the bed. I hug my arms around my knees. My tears soak through the fabric of my clothes.

"Naila?"

The door creaks open. A small slice of light cuts through the darkened room.

"It's me . . ." Selma's voice trails off.

I wipe my tears and shield my face from the sliver of light.

"Are you okay?"

"I'm fine. I'm just feeling homesick. That's all."

Selma sits down next to me in the dark. I look over at her drawn expression. She leans her head back. Her eyes are squeezed shut as though she is fighting tears. I thought telling Selma I was homesick would be a good excuse for my crying, but have I now offended her? I open my mouth to tell her this isn't her fault. That being with her has been the best part of the trip.

But Selma speaks first.

"You found out, didn't you?"

I blink my tears away. "Found out what?"

"You still don't know?" Her voice is soft, but her words hang heavy in the darkness between us.

"Know?" I repeat, looking at her in the darkness.

She says nothing for a moment and then I hear a shudder as a sob escapes her lips.

"Will you forgive me?" Selma looks at the floor, large tears falling down her cheeks.

"Forgive you? What are you talking about? Forgive you for what?"

"They made me swear on Nana's grave I wouldn't tell you." Her body starts shaking with sobs. "I wanted to from the start. I would never keep something like that from anyone, much less you. It's been killing me. When they found out I'd overheard them—"

"Selma!" My voice rises. "Overheard what? What is it?"

"I'm sorry," she pleads. "I should have told you from the beginning."

"It's okay." I drape an arm around her shoulder. "Tell me what happened."

Selma faces me; her eyes are red, and her hands tremble. "You have no idea why your trip got extended?"

"No." I try to keep my voice steady, but my mouth has gone dry.

"You are not going back home."

"I know. We're staying until the end of the summer."

"No. I mean you're not going back, ever."

"Selma, of course I am going back. I know we've stayed longer than we planned, but we're not going to stay here forever. Is that what this is about? I'm sorry I've taken over your room and that you have to go to all these parties because of me, but we're going to leave at the end of the summer. You don't have to worry about that."

"You still don't get it. Can't you tell what is happening?" Her voice wavers. "You have no idea why we suddenly started going to all these dinner parties? Why they always bring their sons when they come to our house? Why their mothers ask you all those questions?"

A hollow darkness descends over me. "Why?"

"It wasn't just your imagination. All those people— they really were there to look at you."

I think back to the gatherings, always with a young man sitting by a parent's side. Suddenly, I gasp, clasping a hand to my mouth. "No." I stare at her. "No. that can't be it."

Selma looks at me. "I overheard my mom talking to your mother about it a few weeks ago. They said you wouldn't be happy about their plans, so no one was supposed to tell you until they found the right person. Your mother said you'd come around to the idea once a good match was found for your husband," Selma says. "That's why everyone cares what you wear. That's what all of this has been about."

Husband.

I can't breathe. I think of my parents, my mother and father's shared glance on the rooftop. My lungs are constricting. Every day they looked into my eyes, every day they smiled at me. Every day they knew. Everyone knew.

"Have they picked someone yet?" I try to remember the men I've seen over the past few weeks, but even the one today is a blurry haze.

"They're considering two right now." She pauses. "I wanted to tell you earlier. They made me swear not to. I just kept hoping and praying your parents would change their minds and see what they were doing, or that you'd somehow find out on your own."

"It's okay." I squeeze her hand. "Just think back, tell me everything you know."

"There was one a few weeks ago who your mother really liked. You might remember him. The one with the mustache and spindly beard? His family lives just two villages over from ours. He's a doctor, and he works in Karachi. His father owns more land than anyone we know. It was a very impressive rishta. His parents want him to settle in the US, but the last time I heard our mothers talking about it, the family was unwilling to budge on the amount they wanted in dowry from your parents."

"And the other one?"

"The other family is looking more serious. They were the ones with the dark green car and the woman with the peacock pendant. Remember? She had that mousy-looking girl next to her with the short haircut. They live in the city, the next one over from our village."

I try thinking back, struggling to visualize. All these weeks, I've been questioned, observed, judged. Offers made. Counteroffers presented.

My chest hurts, but my eyes are dry. Selma tells me more, but it sounds like she's describing someone else's life, not my own. Part of me wants to run as far away as I can, but at the same time, my body feels heavy, bricks attached to my feet.

"The woman with the peacock pendant, she called again this evening," she says quietly. "They're coming again—their son wanted a more proper meeting with you. Nothing has happened yet. But, Naila, something will."

Chapter 21

Just because I am the last to know does not mean anything about my reality has changed. Stay calm. Be still. You'll find a way out of this.

I internalize this mantra, repeating it to myself as I brush my teeth, as I sit at the breakfast table, as I try to eat these eggs that taste like cardboard sliding down my throat. I remind myself of it as I force my mouth to turn upward in the semblance of a smile and push away the other feelings, the darker ones that threaten to engulf me.

"Any calls today?" My mother sits across from me at the breakfast table and looks expectantly at my chachi.

"I think we've had enough visitors," my father says.

"I think you're right." My mother nods. "We could take it easy for a little while at least."

I stiffen, waiting for a guilty glance in my direction, for a clearing of a throat, a moment's hesitation, but my father simply lifts another bite of roti to his mouth.

My mother takes a sip of tea and resumes talking with my chachi.

I feel the small metal outline of the phone in my purse and squeeze it. I need to talk to Saif. I have to tell him. And yet this is where I am stuck. What can I tell him without causing him to panic? And for what? What can he do? I release my grip on the phone. This is something I have to fix myself.

The idea hits with the force of lightning on still water. Standing at the sink washing dishes, I see it like a vision: exactly what I need to do. I dry the dishes and hurry to my bedroom.

"Naila." Selma follows, steps behind me.

"Selma, I'm sorry, but I just want a little privacy."

"Oh, I'm s-sorry," she stammers. "It's just that we haven't really talked about this since last night."

"I know. We'll talk later, but I need a little time to myself right now to think."

"Okay. Well, whatever you need. I'm here to help." She smiles weakly at me before walking away.

I watch her go and feel a twinge of guilt, but I can't draw anyone else into this. I have to do it myself. I can't burden anyone with the potential consequences.

I step into the room. I imagine my mother's horrified

expression, my father's anger. My pace slows to a halt. I don't want to do this, but what else can I do?

I latch the metal lock shut. Yanking open the wooden armoire, I pull out three outfits, tossing them on the bed. The suitcase, wedged awkwardly in the closet, proves more difficult, but after a few sharp tugs, I stagger back with it in hand. My heart races. I stuff in my shoes, my sunglasses and books.

I'm not asking, I remind myself. *I'm telling them.* I've seen cabs come through occasionally. A bus stop can't be too far away. No matter what, I'm leaving. The fear of my parents' reaction threatens to paralyze me, but what keeps me packing, keeps me stuffing things into my suitcase, is the image of the next suitor, watching me with greedy eyes. *No.* I shake my head. *I am out of options.*

I open the outer pouch of my suitcase. I stored two hundred dollars in there before I left for Pakistan, along with my visa and passport. I'm so thankful I never touched this spending money. It's not enough to get me home, but it's enough to get me to the airport. Once I'm there, I'll figure out what to do next.

Wait. I slip my hand inside. Nothing but slick vinyl. *This can't be right.* I had checked the pouch just two weeks ago. I had felt the embossed cover of the passport between my fingers. But now I run my hands through and grasp air.

I push open the cover and peer in. I unzip the suitcase and feel against the lining, between the seams. Nothing.

My knees suddenly feel cold against the hard concrete floor. My money, my visa, my passport, all gone. I grip the edge of the suitcase.

Did they know I would do this? Are they already ten steps ahead?

Chapter 22

The pungent aroma of seven different spices wafts through the house. I hear the sizzling of onions and the patting of dough as I make my way to the kitchen.

I stand at the oval kitchen entrance, watching the women at work. Selma opens the fridge and reaches inside for vegetables. Khala Simki, her back to me, stands by the stove, where she stirs the simmering stew with a wooden spoon.

My mother is at the edge of the counter. I watch her take a ball of dough between her fingers and roll it under her palms until it's thin and round.

"Ami?"

The sounds of the kitchen absorb the word. Clearing my throat, I try again.

"Ami."

My mother looks up. She motions me over with one powdery hand. "I was wondering when you were going to join us! Selma is chopping the vegetables. I could use your help with the tomatoes and onions here."

"I need to talk to you."

"Sure. What is it?"

"I need to talk to you in private."

"I'm in the middle of making roti for dinner."

"This can't wait."

My aunts and Selma look up. My mother gazes at me, apparently cool and calm, though I know she is anything but. One does not speak out of turn, particularly under the watchful eyes of those who will surely dissect your behavior afterward. *Ami,* I think, meeting her gaze, *you must have known I could not stay silent forever.*

"Where is my passport?"

Her eyes widen, but in the next instant, she smiles. "Your passport is with me, of course."

"I need it."

Ami stares at me. Her eyes speak to me much as they have all of my life. "Stop it right now," they say. But today, I simply stare back at her.

She wipes her hands against her apron and walks up to me. Grabbing my elbow, she pulls me toward the empty drawing room. "What was that scene about back there? Have you lost your mind?"

"I need my passport. My visa. My money. They were all

in my suitcase. Now they're gone." I refuse to look at her.

"I put all our passports together, for safekeeping. Why the sudden need for it?"

"I'm leaving."

"Leaving?" She crosses her arms. "How interesting. And where, pray tell, are you leaving to?"

"I'm going back home." I push down the lump growing thick in my throat. "You both said no, but I have to go. I have things to do at home."

"Is this not a home to you too? Haven't your aunts and uncles treated you like a daughter? Your younger cousins absolutely adore you. Selma is like your sister. Yet you want so badly to leave."

"I appreciate everything everyone has done for me, but it's time for me to go. I need my passport, my wallet, my visa."

"I could tell you were beginning to get unstable." My mother wipes her forehead with her shawl. "But I never thought you would consider bringing this much shame on us."

"This has nothing to do with shame, Ami. I need to go home, that's all."

"Who are you, Naila? I raised you from a baby, but I don't recognize you anymore. It's him, isn't it? You want to go back to him, right?"

"No. My passport." My voice cracks. "I just want my passport."

"You're not getting it. It's safe with us. Please." She meets my gaze. "Please trust us."

I watch her leave and press a trembling hand against the wall.

How can I explain any of this to Saif, I wonder, when I can't make sense of it myself?

Chapter 23

The sun has barely risen when Khala Simki taps on my door and pops her head inside. "When Nasim comes for lunch today, please wear the green salwar kamiz I bought for you." Before I can respond, she's gone.

Selma is already sitting up in her bed, watching me.

"Is this the one they're serious about?" I ask her.

"Yes. Remember the woman with the peacock pendant? It's her family."

"I can't do it, Selma." My heart hammers in my chest. "I can't sit there and pretend I don't know."

"Do they know yet that I told you?"

"Selma, I will never tell them you told me, I swear."

"I want to help you." Her eyes well with tears. "I should have told you from the beginning, but I'll help you. I'll do whatever it takes."

"I don't need help."

"But you do. Let's go for a walk today, talk about

things. I have some ideas, but I don't want to talk about anything in the house."

"Maybe later." I open the armoire. I know I'm hurting her by shutting her out, but I know it's for her own good. The more Selma knows, the more trouble she will be in later. I yank the green outfit from the armoire, snapping the hanger in two with my force. The thought of sitting down for this meeting makes me sick, but until I know what to do, I must pretend I know nothing.

There is a knock on the front door. My mother grips me by the wrist, leading me into the drawing room. "Sit with me. Selma will make chai today."

I take a seat next to her on the white sofa. The guests walk in. Their footsteps echo off the walls. I keep my gaze fixed on my coral bangles, twisting the thin scarf resting in my lap with my fingers. I wind it so tight, my fingertips turn pink, then white.

I don't want to marry you. I want to scream this as I hear them settle in on the sofa across from me. For a moment I'm struck by the impulse to do just this. To stand up and scream at everyone in this room, to humiliate my parents as they are humiliating me—but what good will it do? All of these people gathered in this room are coconspirators against me. Why would any of them care if I disagreed? I squeeze my hands until they go numb.

I try to focus on other things. The sugar-coated biscuits on the coffee table. The glow of the sun filtering through the translucent red curtains. But I can't forget he's here. I can't forget he's watching me.

It takes everything in me to fight the urge to run out of the room, the desire growing stronger with each passing moment I spend sitting under his stare. I know what he is doing. I can tell in the way he shifts his weight and clears his throat. He wants me to look at him. Though curiosity pokes its head and nudges me to meet his gaze, I refuse. I will not give him the satisfaction.

I hear his mother, her voice a low soprano in the quiet room. I close my eyes. I think of Saif. His smile, his dimple, the way he holds my hand before kissing me. He is the only thing keeping me from what I fear would otherwise be the slow onset of insanity.

"We must be on our way," the woman finally says. I hear the creaks of the sofa as people move to stand, murmurs of thanks and good-bye. I look up just then to see my father laughing, patting my chacha's shoulder. He walks down the hall in his favorite salwar kamiz and the dark vest he wears every day without fail, despite the heat and humidity. My eyes widen. I press a hand against my purse. Just as I refuse to part with my purse, he refuses to part with his vest.

I know exactly what I need to do.

Night passes slowly as I wait for everyone to fall asleep. Finally, I slip out of the bedroom and make my way down the hall. My bare feet feel cool against the floor. I pause at my parents' shut bedroom door and press my ear against it. Silence. Turning the knob, I open it a crack before slipping in. The moonlight casts a gentle glow on my mother's sleeping figure, tucked under the white sheet. Her eyes are closed, her lips parted. My father, too, is sound asleep, exhaling deep, guttural snores.

I searched this room just hours ago, every suitcase flap, beneath every pillow and mattress. I have to find his vest; there's no other place my passport could possibly be.

I drop to my hands and knees and crawl to the closet. I press my hands to the cold metal surface and push the accordion door with my finger, trying to nudge it open. It doesn't budge. I tug again and cringe. This time it groans loudly, and then, a thud. An avalanche of books come tumbling down.

"Naila?"

My father sits up in bed, rubbing his eyes. I stay still,

half crouched on the floor. *It's a bad dream,* I think frantically. *Please go to sleep.*

A click, and suddenly the room fills with yellow artificial light.

"What is it? Is everything okay?! Is someone hurt?" My mother is sitting bolt upright, her hair matted against her face. She looks down at me and puts a hand to her chest. "What's wrong?"

I look at my father's confused expression. I watch my mother tie her hair up in a haphazard bun. I can't breathe. Who are these parents? Why are their expressions unreadable despite a lifetime of presumed literacy? No matter how much they disapprove of Saif, no matter how angry they are, I do not deserve this.

"What am I doing? What are *you* doing?" My voice pierces the quiet room. "Why are you doing this?"

In an instant, my father is in front of me, his hand pressed against my mouth. "Enough," he says into my ear. "No tamasha here. Not in the middle of the night."

I try to wrench his hands away, but he holds me tightly. "I know what you're trying to do!" I scream through the palm he has pressed against my face. "I know everything!"

My mother stands up and looks out the window. Her body trembles. I watch her contorted face; she's crying.

I stop struggling. My father releases his grip. I press my

hands against my eyes. "Ami. Please. Please. Don't do this to me."

"No," my mother says softly. "We would never want to hurt you. We don't have a choice, though. We've lost you."

"You're gone, beta." My father's face is no longer stern—he looks familiar again, like the father I had before my life shattered. "We have to help bring you back. We're your parents. It's our responsibility."

"You don't have to bring me back. I'm not gone. Just look at me. I'm right here, I'm your daughter."

"But you *are* gone, and it breaks our heart that you can't see it."

"Ami, I know I've made mistakes. I'm sorry. I am so sorry. But I've done nothing to deserve this."

Ami clutches a gray chador tight around her shoulders. "When you were little, we could just hide the cookies you wanted. We could send you to your room to consider what you did. We did what we thought was right. We tried to raise you well."

"You did raise me well." Fat tears roll down my face in a steady torrent.

"We raised you well?" My mother laughs. "We can see for ourselves what a job we did. We are your parents. We love you. We want what's best for you. If we see you doing wrong, we have to stop you. Even if you hate us, and I know you do right now, one day, you will see we did what was best for you. That is what we have always tried to do."

I look at my parents. I can try all I want to, I realize. But I will never convince them.

I make my way back to my room. My body feels numb. I walk inside and shut the door behind me, trying to still my trembling frame.

"Selma, wake up."

She wakes with a start. "What's wrong?"

"Selma, I need your help." Tears slip down my face. "I need to tell you everything."

Chapter 24

The wind blows overhead in the sugarcane field, whipping through the canes but providing little relief from the heat baking the earth as we walk through them. We've spent quite a few days here together, but this time feels different. The stalks, in shades of green with flecks of white, stretch row upon row on either side of us. We've never walked so deep into the fields before, and I've never felt quite this jittery. I keep glancing over my shoulders, flinching at the rustle of the leaves or the faint sounds of voices in the distance. I'm overwhelmed today by the expanse of my chacha's farmland. There is no end in sight. How far would I have to run if I tried to escape?

I look at Selma. She nods. Both of us sit down on a patch of open grassy field. I pull out my phone and flip it open, dialing the number.

"Naila. Is it you?"

"Saif." I open my mouth to say more, but his voice reminds me afresh of what I have to tell him. Selma grips my hand. I take a deep breath, explaining everything for the first time.

"So now"—my voice trembles—"my parents know I want to leave. They caught me trying to get my passport."

"I've been going crazy these past few days. I didn't know what was going on, but I knew something was very wrong. Have they picked someone yet?"

"Someone came yesterday. It might be serious."

"This can't be happening. I can't believe this. Are they planning a . . . wedding?"

"I don't know. I think so. Maybe an engagement now and a wedding later. At least that's what I'm hoping."

"No. They've got it all planned out. If you come back, they know you'll find a way out of it. No, they're going to make sure you stay. They're going to make sure they ruin your life well and good while they have you in their grip."

"I don't know what to do, Saif."

He's silent for a few moments. "I'll call the US Embassy in Pakistan," he finally says. "I think they're in Islamabad. When I tell them you're being held against your will, I'm sure they'll have a procedure to get you out of there. Keep your phone on you. I'll text you as soon as I hear something—and, Naila"—his voice softens— "everything will be okay. Pretend like you're the happiest person in the world until you hear from me. We'll get through this."

The next morning, I check my phone: *Call ASAP.*

"What's wrong?" Selma sits across from me on the bed.

I show her the text message. She walks to the door and locks it.

"Call him," she says. "We can't wait until this afternoon."

I move to the farthest end of the room and dial his number.

"Naila," he says in a rushed voice, "you have to go to the embassy. It's in Islamabad. I told them everything. They said they can help, but you have to go to them."

Blood rushes to my face. "Saif, how am I supposed to get there?"

"I know. I know. I told them to come get you, that you were trapped, but they said they can't." He takes a deep breath. "You have to get to them. You have to."

"There's no way for me to get there. Things are different here. It's not so simple."

"Talk to Selma. Maybe she can give you some advice. If you don't go there, they can't help you, and you have to get out of there. Now."

I hang up the phone. Back home, this would be less complicated. But here, I may as well plan a trip to the moon.

"What did he say?"

"I have to go to Islamabad. I have to get to the embassy." The phone rests in my lap. I tuck my knees under me. "It's just as simple as that, right?"

"My father goes all the time to Islamabad. Most of our fabrics come from there."

"Your dad has a car. We drove in it here from the airport. I know where he keeps the key. I'm sure I could figure out how to use it."

"It's the loudest car ever invented," she reminds me. "Even if you got it out of the garage unwatched, as soon as you turned the corner, everyone would see you."

"I've seen taxis."

"Hardly ever," Selma says. "I wouldn't know how to track one down. Besides, taxis don't travel that far—they go from village to village when they do, and they would definitely think twice before taking you anywhere."

I think of the horse-drawn carriages, the rickshaws belching smoke with each sputter. Desperately I even consider walking, but I know none of these will work, none of these can help me escape.

"What about a bus?" I finally ask.

Selma claps her hands. "Yes! It's not in this village, but it can't be too far away. Probably in the next town over. I know people who've taken it. I think my mother has a black burka somewhere in her closet. She never wears it, so she won't even notice it's missing. It will cover you up from head to toe, and in the dark no one will think you're anyone except someone's grandmother. I'm sure one of the buses will take you to Islamabad."

I feel deflated. "So you don't know which bus goes to Islamabad?"

"No, but I'm sure we can figure that out."

"I'll just have to see if I can find some money to get me there. My parents took all the money I brought with me."

"Don't worry about the money." Selma points to a wooden box on the dresser. "I have been saving all my holiday money, birthdays, my eidi, since I was eight years old. I have enough."

"Listen"—my voice shakes—"when they realize I'm gone and what happened, you need to tell them I stole it from you, okay? They're going to assume you helped me. If anything happened to you because of me, I would never forgive myself."

"No one knows about the money. They won't know I helped you."

"I don't care if you have to badmouth me, call me names. Promise me you will make sure they won't find out you helped me, okay?"

Selma nods. "I promise."

❋ ❋ ❋

I slide on my blue sandals and leave the house with Selma the next morning. "Bring back some tomatoes from the market!" calls my chachi as we unlock the front door. My chachi walks up to Selma and hands her money. "Don't be home too late. You girls seem to live out there these days."

Clouds provide no relief on this bright sunny day. Within seconds of stepping onto the road, thick beads of sweat form on my forehead.

Selma holds a hand over her eyes and squints. "Mustafa Sahib will know which bus goes where. Work your magic with him." She grins. I roll my eyes and laugh.

Mustafa, a short stout man with a thick head of black hair and a thicker mustache, leans on his metal cart under a shaded tree. He perks up as he sees us approach and reaches into his freezer, pulling out two pistachio kulfis.

"Nahin," protests Mustafa as I hand him money. "Why do you always give me a little more? This isn't done here, you know."

"It's a tip—please take it."

He smiles, stuffing the extra change into his pocket.

"I noticed most people here don't have cars. How do you get to the big cities?" It's a simple question from an Amriki girl. Still, my body tenses, waiting for his eyes to narrow, for his smile to fade.

Mustafa brushes a sticky hand against his shirt. "Most

of us aren't as lucky as your chacha. We can't afford fancy cars, but we take the bus."

"The bus. I haven't seen a station here."

"Nahin." He waves his hand. "You just take a rickshaw or tonga over to the next town over—it's five or six kilometers that way." He points toward a road. "It's easy. Fifteen minutes, and I'm at the bus station heading to Islamabad." He winks at me. "Maybe you can convince your chacha to loan me his car? Would make my life a lot easier."

I take a bite of the quickly melting kulfi and do my best to appear simply curious and conversational.

"In America, the buses have machines where you just put in your money and your ticket pops out. They even make them with air-conditioning and bathrooms."

He laughs. "I see your movies from America. I see your trains and your buses. This is not a bus like that. This bus is not for a girl like you! No. It is a big metal thing, and there is not one seat for each person. There are many people on the bus. Sometimes when you're going town to town, people even sit on the roof. If you want to see the big cities of Pakistan and get out of this boring little village, tell your chacha to take you in his car."

Chapter 25

I'm OK.

I tuck my phone back into my purse. I hear Imran's laughter bounce off the walls. My younger cousins run back and forth outside in the hallway, arguing and squealing in the same breath. How many days have Selma and I spent planning and mapping out each aspect of my escape? How can everything still seem so perfectly normal?

I get up. I don't want to leave the room, but I know I have to act normal. Just then, Selma steps inside—her face is drawn, her eyes downcast.

"They're coming tomorrow."

"Again?" I ask. "Can't they just leave me alone for a little while?"

"I overheard Phupo arguing with my mom." She swallows. "They want to set the wedding date."

The wedding date. My knees threaten to buckle.

"Your parents were there this afternoon. At their house. When they said they were going to visit an old friend for lunch, that's what they were talking about. Tomorrow those people are bringing a gold set"—her voice breaks—"for your engagement."

I want to say something, but nothing comes out.

"Phupo is furious no one told you. She's threatening to do it herself. My mom said your mother will tell you tomorrow, before they come."

"They're going to tell me?" My voice rises. I scarcely recognize it. "I can't do that! I can't sit there and pretend to go along with it. What am I going to do?"

"What we knew you would have to do sooner or later. You have to go."

"Tonight?"

"Yes. I never really thought you would leave me until today. I guess I secretly hoped things would get better, but now we know that's not going to happen. It's best to leave tonight. When it's safest."

I embrace Selma. My heart feels heavy. I think of Imran. I will hug him tonight. He'll roll his eyes and laugh at me while I blink back tears. Will I ever see him again? I have no choice. I have to do this.

Selma goes to her dresser and pulls out a thick envelope. She sits next to me and turns it onto the bed.

Clumps of colorful money fall out. After counting it, she hands it to me.

"There should be enough for the bus ride and, hopefully, for some food and a taxi."

I look at the money in my hands.

I will pay the money back one day, tenfold. But I know I can never really repay her.

Not for the grave risk she is taking for me.

Chapter 26

I watch my father reclining on the sofa; his hands rest on his stomach. He's talking to my chacha, who sits across from him. My mother sits on patterned cushions in the corner of the living room with my aunts. Imran rests his elbow on the coffee table. He's playing carrom board with Sohail. They flick the pieces on the tray back and forth, boasting about who will win.

Will this be the last time I see them all? I look at my mother's profile. Tonight is the last night she will look at me as her daughter. The moment I leave tonight, I will lose all of this, but what other choice do I have? My throat constricts. I stand up.

"Where are you going?" my mother asks.

"I'm tired. I'm going to lie down."

"It's not even ten yet." She raises an eyebrow. "Are you feeling okay?"

"I didn't sleep well last night. The kids woke me up early."

"Your cousins cannot get enough of you, but they really should let you rest. Go ahead, then. I want to take you shopping tomorrow morning."

I walk away quickly so she can't see my expression.

I lie in bed, waiting. Slowly the noises in the distance grow soft, then faint. I hear my chachi's footsteps. She is shutting off lights and closing doors. Then, nothing.

Selma gets up first. She heads to the closet and pulls out an empty, worn book bag. I pull out the bottom drawer of Selma's dresser and remove the dried dates, fruit, and small containers of water I pilfered through the course of the day.

Mustafa's directions were abstract, but I'm certain if I keep following the road he showed me, it will eventually take me there. Slipping out of my clothes, I fling them on the bed and pull on a T-shirt and a pair of jeans. I grab the folded burka and put it on.

"Remember, walk calmly and quietly. No one can see you in the dark, but if they notice you before you leave this village, they'll know something is up."

I adjust the book bag under my burka. "Is it time? Should I go now?" The plan seemed so concrete in my mind, but now I'm starting to panic. I push out the images of my parents, their expressions when they discover I'm gone.

"It's time."

I pull her to me and hold on tight, fighting tears. She hugs me back. Neither of us speaks. There's nothing more to say.

I open the bedroom door and step into the hallway. One of my cousins is sleeping on a charpay in the family room. I hear sheets rustle and freeze. He shifts sides and, in a few seconds, resumes snoring.

I walk to the front door, its hand-carved designs obscured in the night. I graze my hand against it, feeling for the lock, and then press. My heart pounds loudly, drumming in my ears. I practiced opening and unlocking this door for days. It opens now, quickly and silently.

The courtyard looks so inviting during the day, but now the potted plants seem ominous, their shadows leering at me. I make my way to the brick wall and pull the latch to the metal gate; it opens with a creak. I look back at the house, a large gray brick building blending into the night. I turn and slip through the gate.

I feel the familiar road under my feet as I try making sense of my surroundings. I've seen this road so many times before, but right now in the dark, deserted, the storefronts covered with large sheets of metal, everything seems unfamiliar. I take a deep breath, trying to regain my composure. My chacha's fields to the left, which normally seem inviting, a cool place for reprieve in the unyielding summer, are ominous in the night. There is no one in sight, and yet I feel watched with each step I take, as if things are hiding, crouching alongside the road.

I pick up my pace. The air in the burka grows warmer, but I don't stop. It doesn't matter if my feet begin to ache or bleed; turning back is no longer an option.

Once I make it to the bus station and board the bus, I will be safe.

Chapter 27

The engine cranks until the bus reaches a loud, self-doubting hum before it jerks forward. Aside from one elderly toothless lady several rows ahead of me, I am the only woman here. Old men and young boys cram together in every spot but leave the space next to me unoccupied. They seem exhausted. Their eyes are closed, their bodies still.

The bus trembles as it turns onto another country road, sunrise slowly filtering into the world. With each creak and groan, my anxiety dissipates. I don't know where I'm going or what I will do when I arrive, but the nightmare is behind me.

My mother is probably waking up right now. When will she knock on my bedroom door? When will she ask me to hurry up so we can go shopping? When will she realize I am gone? *No.* I push these thoughts from my mind. It does no good to question the past. I have to keep moving forward now.

I don't know how I fall asleep. Maybe the weeks of sleep-lessness finally catch up to me, along with the hypnotic rumbling of the bus, but I wake with a start. My fore-head slams into the seat in front of me. Other passengers stumble forward, toppling on one another. I'm watching people rearrange themselves and their belongings when suddenly I hear a loud commotion outside. The driver exits the bus. The loud, angry voices grow louder with each passing second. Just then, the men at the front of the bus step aside as someone pushes through. I look at their anxious expressions. Have we been hijacked? *They can take my money*—but I stiffen at the thought of my cell phone. *They can't have that.*

All thoughts vanish when I see the man walking down the bus. He parts the crowd with his girth. His face is beet red, his jaw hard. His breathing is ragged and hoarse.

It's my chacha.

No, I think, my eyes struggling to register him. *It can't be him. Not here, not now.*

He scans each row. *I'm not here,* I pray. *Leave this veiled woman alone.* He slows as he passes my seat. I close my eyes. In that moment, I want nothing more than for death to swoop in with its claws and wrench me away.

But death, in the form I desire—my soul painlessly exiting my body—does not come.

Since forming the plan, I've imagined my capture on many sleepless nights. Men with flashlights chasing me down dark streets. Sleepy faces staring at me in shock as I unlocked the front door of my home in a dark burka. Neighbors sitting on a porch stoop, calling my name in the dead of night. Yet never had I imagined that they would find me here, on the bus to safety. This was how I escaped.

Yet as unceremoniously as a goat that wandered too close to the street before being fully branded, I'm yanked from my seat, dragged down the aisle, down the rough metal steps.

Instincts spring to life. I kick, twist my wrists to pry myself away from him. I bite his arm. He does not let go.

The bus driver and passengers watch my uncle shove me into the car.

"*Help me!*" I scream out before he clamps his hand tightly on my mouth. I watch the bus shrink into nothingness in the distance.

Chapter 28

I remember the first time I stepped into this bedroom. Selma's room felt so large. Two twin beds on opposite ends of the room with handwoven quilts of different textures and colors. Beige paint cracking along the edges of the ceiling. I remember seeing the iron bars on the windows for the first time. They made me feel safe, secure from the outside world. Now, as I press my back against the cold wall, this room feels small and narrow, closing in on me. The bars' purpose is finally clear.

My father stands before me, his face a deep shade of red. Sweat trickles down his brow. He walks toward me with deliberate steps. I stare at him. This man seems a stranger. I look into his eyes. Has he forgotten the bicycle lessons in the park near our house? The bandage he applied when I fell and scraped my knee? How could this person who raised me with so much love be the person standing before me?

"Where is it?"

He is mere inches from me. I can feel his anger, a solid, tangible thing; it reverberates through the room. It makes me tremble.

"I want the phone. Give it to me."

I keep my face blank, thankful I hid it quickly once they shoved me into this room.

"There is no phone."

"No phone?" He stares at me. "Is this who you've become? You who can look me in the eyes and lie to me like this? This isn't my daughter. My daughter would never so willfully go against everything we ever taught her. I raised you better than this."

"Don't do this," I plead. "Please, don't do this to me."

"To you? Look what you are doing to us!" His voice catches. "For generations my family lived in this village. People looked up to us. They came to us to resolve their disputes. And now? The respect we built up over the generations, you are trying to ruin all of it!"

I know I will forget many details of this moment, but I will never forget the slap across my face. Or my chacha storming inside, my hands upon the cold concrete floor, the metallic taste of blood in my mouth. I know I will remember the overturned mattresses, the clothing flung from the closet, and the moment my father's hand grazes the cushion by the bed, pulling out the purse—and my phone. I will never forget the way he walked out of the room, locking the door behind him and throwing away the key to the life I could have had.

Chapter 29

"She's not eating."

"Make her eat, then."

"She's asking for Selma or Imran. She said she will eat if she can see one of them."

"Who is she to make demands of us? It's this indulgent attitude her parents tolerated that has led to the problem we have today."

"It won't hurt for them to come in for just a few minutes."

"We're not playing this game. Go in there and make her eat, or I will."

The door opens, casting a pale glow into the dimly lit room.

"Naila." My phupo walks up to me and kneels beside me. "I brought your favorite food—look, kebobs, rice. And here, I brought you some Coke."

I don't move from my spot in the corner of the

room; my arms hug my knees. I can't remember how many days it's been, and I am beyond the point of caring. My stomach grumbles, but I feel no hunger. *Where's Selma?* I want to ask. *What did they do to her? Where is she?* But I know it does no good to ask. I screamed her name through the door the first few days until my voice went hoarse. No one responded. Sometimes, like now, I wonder if Selma ever really existed. Perhaps she is just a figment of my imagination.

"Beta," Phupo pleads, "you need to eat. You can't survive like this." With a fork, she cuts off a piece of kebob and dangles it by my mouth. I turn my head away.

"What's happening is wrong." She leans closer to me. "I don't blame you for running away, but nothing can be done now. Don't make this harder for yourself. Please, eat something. Don't do this to yourself."

I continue staring down at the gray concrete floor.

Phupo slides the plate toward me and gently cups my face. "I'm leaving the plate here. Please eat it tonight. Starving yourself isn't going to change anything."

The next morning, Phupo sighs when she sees the untouched, cold food.

I hear voices outside the door.

"She didn't eat anything. This is the fifth day. She's wasting away."

"I told you it does no good to sweet-talk her. I told you what we should have done from the start. Now I'm in charge."

I don't flinch when my chacha walks into the room. He slams a tray of food on the ground. He takes in my unkempt hair, my tearstained face, and my lips pressed together in silent defiance.

A loud click. "I don't have the time nor the patience to deal with you," he says. "My brother made the mistake of getting greedy and running off to America without any concern for the family he left behind. You can't help what you are. But you brought my daughter into this, and that I will never forgive." He breaks off a piece of kebob from the tray. "Either you will eat, or I will make you eat. The choice is yours."

I keep my mouth in a thin line, tightly closed.

"Then you have made your decision." He leans toward me and roughly pries my lips open, shoving the food into my mouth. I gag as he picks up a glass of water and pours the drink down my throat. I cough at the strange, bitter aftertaste, but he doesn't stop until the glass is empty.

I bend over, heaving; water trickles down my chin. Almost instantly, I feel hazy. The drink. He's drugging me,

I realize. I try to get up, but a rush of heaviness settles over me.

"Keep resisting, and I will come back here every single time." A dullness settles over me. I watch him walk away. The door slams with finality behind him.

Chapter 30

"Where am I going?" I ask my mother and Khala Simki. This is my first time outside the bedroom since I tried to leave. The world seems orange through the gauzy veil draped over my head. They grip me by my shoulders, steadying my feet, leading me toward the cushioned center of the room.

"Just rest," Khala Simki says.

I fold my hands, suppressing a yawn. I sit down cross-legged and lean against a soft cushion. It feels like a cloud. I sleep all the time lately. Even when I'm awake, my brain feels clouded. I try fighting it, but I can't. Life is a dull echo while I sit in a vacuum of darkness.

I look up when I hear the rhythmic sound of drums, and a group of women singing songs. Young girls I recognize from the village are dancing to recorded music on the stereo in bright red, green, and yellow dresses on the open space just feet from where I sit.

A tiny woman in a mustard yellow outfit sits in front of me. I know her. I've seen her on walks through the village toting a toddler with a shock of brown hair. She grips my hand firmly in hers, stretching the palm taut, a cone of henna in the other hand. I watch her paint my hand with the focus and precision of a surgeon. I try to meet her gaze, but she seems oblivious to the fact that the hand she's painting is connected to me.

The swirls, cool to my skin, spiral into flowers, peacocks, and stars traveling the length of my arm, and then I watch as she begins on my feet. My mother and I painted our hands with henna just like this growing up. We dipped toothpicks in bowls of cool brown henna and traced spiraling clouds and tulips across our palms. None of our designs were ever quite as beautiful as these. I want to ask what the occasion is tonight, a holiday, a wedding, but the fogginess is too heavy.

And who is to say this isn't a dream? I rest against the cushions.

"It's okay," my chachi whispers. "You can go to sleep if you want."

I startle and look over at her. "I'm tired," I tell her. "I'm so tired."

"Here, drink this." She hands me a glass of water. "Then just lean back and rest. You don't have to do anything but sit and look pretty."

"Pretty?" I ask, but my aunt simply pats my shoulder. There's so much more I want to ask her, but my words are too heavy. Everything is too heavy. I lean back against the cushions and sleep.

The next day, a thicker veil covers my face. Everything is blurred and hazy. I am in my parents' bedroom, seated on the edge of their bed. People surround me from all sides, hands holding me firmly in their grip.

My clothes are suffocating me. Maroon velvet with gold and green embroidery. The heavy fabric clings to my body, but the veil, with its thick handwork, hangs heavier still upon my head. I tried to stop them from placing it on me, but deliberate hands gripped me on each side as they pinned the veil in place, thrust a gold necklace with rubies around my neck, and put on large gold earrings that weigh down my ears like anchors.

Khala Simki's high-pitched laugh floats through the air. Her bangles clink like wind chimes and then, the melodic voice of the imam whose voice echoes daily from the local minaret sounds so clear, it's as if he's right here in this room. I try to focus on his words, but they feel slippery. I can't grasp them, and no matter how hard I try, I can't formulate words of my own.

"Naila Rehman," he says, "do you accept?"

Accept? Accept what?

He lets out a ragged cough. "Naila Rehman, do you accept this marriage?"

Marriage?

My mouth goes dry. I struggle against the foggy sensation enveloping me that's prevented me from understanding any of this. Until now.

This is a wedding.

This is my wedding.

A table is placed in front of me with a long white paper and blue pen.

"Do you accept?" he asks again.

"No," I tell him. Warm tears trail down my face. "I don't accept this. No."

No one replies.

Did I say these words out loud? Or am I simply imagining all of this? Maybe this is just a bad dream I can't escape.

I try standing up, but rough hands shove me back down. Thick hands push the pen toward me. I flatten my palm, but someone pushes my hands together, forcing my fingers around the pen. Gripped by the elbow, pushed down at the shoulders, I watch my hand make motions, incoherent ink writing out the semblance of a name. My name.

The pen falls from my hands. I hear loud voices and laughter.

The hands that held me loosen their grip; my arms fall limp to my sides.

I look up. My stomach lurches. The room seems to tilt. A crowd of people swirl in and out of my line of vision. I see my chachi in pink. Khala Simki with a strained smile on her powder-white face.

Where's Selma?

Where's Imran?

People brush past me, embracing one another. Nobody is looking at me. Nobody seems to notice I am even here.

On the bed, my hands shake. *What just happened? What have they done to me?*

Part Two

Chapter 31

The room in this unfamiliar home is frosty cool as I sit upon the bed. After a hazy car ride, my aunts deposited me here, positioning me in the center, spreading the folds of my red lengha around me, folding my hennaed hands one upon the other. A canopy of strung petals surrounds me.

A wall clock ticks loudly at the far end of this room. The ornate white wooden furniture in this large room is painted with pink flowers and green petals, as are the oversized nightstands and dressers. I keep my gaze fixed on my hands, trying not to listen to the loud voices and laughter outside the room.

"Mubarak!" A female voice offers congratulations. "The wedding couldn't have gone better!"

"So traditional. I heard she was from America, but you wouldn't know it from the way she acts," says another.

"Really, Nasim, she is beautiful. You got it all with your new daughter-in-law!"

I want to feel something. Here in the privacy of this room, I should feel something: anger, panic, fear. Yet nothing comes to the surface. *Maybe,* I think, *if I don't look up, if I simply look down and never look up again for the rest of my life, the feelings buried within will never rise to the surface.* I can accept the numbness instead of the madness that could follow.

The voices outside the room grow louder. Footsteps approach and then—the door opens. I don't flinch when it shuts. A lock turns.

But for his movement, silence envelops the room, amplifying his steps and the rustling sound of his kamiz as he walks. I sense him near me. I keep my eyes fixed on my hands, squeezing them tightly. I look at my bracelets. The room grows perceptibly cooler.

He sits down. The bed shifts. I feel him next to me. Looking at me. My head feels heavy. Black spots dot my vision.

He leans close to me. I can feel his breath against my skin.

"May I lift your veil?"

I raise my eyes and see his hands, one on either side of my veil. He lifts it and drapes it around my shoulders. I stare at these hands, the long tan fingers. Suddenly, I recoil. The reality of this moment opens its palm and slaps me across my face: *Whose hands are these?*

I look up at the eyes looking back at me. A young man wearing a cream-colored outfit and a white turban is watching me. His face is darker than mine. His eyes are deep brown. I stare into this stranger's eyes, his intense gaze penetrating me.

I feel dizzy.

The black spots dotting my vision multiply.

I feel heavy, like I am made of lead. Every wall I held up, every ounce of strength I maintained to fight this inevitability now comes crashing down.

My next memory is one of coldness. A cool towel pressed upon my forehead. I keep my eyes closed and pray my eyes will open to my house and my twin-sized bed that looks out at the crepe myrtle in our Florida yard.

When I look up, my new reality hits me full force. He presses the towel to my head. When he sees my eyes flutter open, he takes a deep breath.

"Thank God, you're awake."

I try to sit up, but he places a hand on my shoulder. "Shh . . . lie down, close your eyes. It's been a long day for both of us, but even longer for you, I'm sure. You need rest." He reaches across the bed and removes a pillow. I watch him come close to me. He lifts my head and places the pillow underneath. He drapes a white sheet over me.

I watch him walk back to the head of the four-poster bed and take another pillow. Walking to a sofa in the corner of the bedroom, he sits down, placing the pillow on one end. He walks to a closet and pulls out a floral blanket. I watch him lay it on the sofa as well.

I dare not make a move, afraid that if he looks at me again, this small act of kindness will vanish. He walks to the front of the room and turns off the lights. I wait until I hear the sofa creak with his weight before I close my eyes.

Chapter 32

The thick beige curtains keep the room shaded. Voices echo off the tiled floor just outside.

"Amin, is she coming out? It's almost noon. Saba set the table over an hour ago, and I spent all morning cooking. Everything is getting cold."

"I'm sure she'll be out in a minute. It was a long day yesterday."

"Still, look at all this food, the cholay, halvah, nihari . . . You know, the butcher gave me such a hard time. I really wanted to serve everything warm. It won't be tasty otherwise."

"I'll go check on her."

I shut my eyes and draw my covers over myself. The door opens and shuts. I hear another person, her voice sharp.

"She's taking her sweet time, isn't she?"

"Stop that," replies the woman. "She's a bride. It can

take some time to get dressed. Help me put these pots on the stove. Just a little heat, and they will be warm again."

Footsteps approach the bed.

"Naila?"

I clench my jaw.

"Are you okay?" He tilts his head. "Feeling better?"

I say nothing. There is nothing to say.

"Well, um, I hope you are." He clears his throat. "Brunch is ready. We would love it if you could join us."

He stands at the foot of the bed and grips the corner post. He looks at me with a hesitant smile. "Should I tell her you will be out in a few minutes?"

No, I want to tell him. *I want you to leave me alone. I want you all to just disappear.* But I can't say any of this. Not until I know my next step.

A small gasp emerges when I enter the dining room fifteen minutes later. I look up. Three women stare back at me. They take in my wrinkled cotton clothing, the shawl draped around my shoulders, the brown slippers on my feet.

Amin's mother, Nasim, stares at me before shaking her head. "Come join us. It's our first meal as a family." She points to an empty chair. Amin sits next to me.

She introduces me to everyone sitting around the table. Saba, her daughter, who I now recognize from earlier meetings at my uncle's home, is seated to her left. Her reddish-brown hair is cut in a short bob. She rests one bony hand under her severe chin and watches me, unsmiling. Feiza, the other daughter-in-law, is seated on the other side with a little girl in her arms. Feiza's hair is long and braided; loose tendrils frame her pretty oval face and large eyes, which watch me with curiosity now.

"My son Usman was not able to make it to the wedding," Nasim says. She sits down across from me. "But you'll meet him when he comes at the end of the month for his break."

I fix my gaze on the table linens. My foggy state is wearing off bit by bit, and I am sad to see it go.

"Naila, you're not eating anything." Nasim reaches over and takes my empty white plate. She places a freshly tossed puri and a spoon of cholay and brown halva on it. I tug the warm bread with my fingers and swirl the food on my plate.

"Some relatives are coming by today to meet you," she says. "Choose any outfit from the ones we've given you. Our servant can iron it for you if needed." I feel her watching me, waiting for a response, but I keep looking down at the steaming food on my plate.

"Or," Nasim rushes on, "Feiza and Saba can help you pick out an outfit and matching jewelry. I'm sure you're overwhelmed. The wedding happened much sooner than we all thought it would."

"We are very happy you are a part of our family now."

I look up at these words. It's Amin. He's watching me with a small smile on his lips.

Saif.

His image comes unbidden to my mind, seizing me with such suddenness, I'm afraid I might be sick. I look away and swallow. I press a hand to my side, but of course, my purse is gone.

He must be calling. Texting. He must be worried beyond belief. He has no idea what happened.

"What about this one?" Feiza lifts a pink outfit with gold sequins. "Nasim picked this one out herself—she thought it suited your complexion. You are very fair, so much fairer than me." She blushes at this and looks down.

I sit down on the bed. Her daughter toddles up to me. She tugs my kamiz and babbles incoherently.

"Zaina likes you." Feiza smiles. "She never goes to anyone like that."

Zaina climbs into my lap. I smile, and somehow the act of moving my lips upward makes my stomach hurt. A tear slips down my cheek.

"Oh, I know. I know it's hard." She comes up to me

and puts a hand on my shoulder. "I got married three years ago, and I still miss my parents so much. But you'll see them again. I know Nasim was saying you could go back to see them in two weeks, before they leave to return to America."

My throat constricts at her words. *Return to America.*

"It's going to be okay. I know what you're going through." She sits next to me on the bed and pats my hand.

How can you possibly know, I want to ask, *when I myself can't make sense of any of this?*

"Don't you look nice," his mother says when I exit the bedroom. "See? This is how a bride should look. Come, let me show you around your new home."

"I can come too." Amin makes his way toward us.

"Nonsense." Nasim bats a hand at him. "This is my one-on-one time with our new bride."

I trail behind her as she leads the way. "My husband, may he rest in peace, put a lot of care into making this a special house. Everything is up-to-date and modern. It cost a lot of money, but you can see that it looks like houses you have in America." Nasim opens the dark wooden cabinets of the kitchen, showing me plates, sugar, and spices.

We walk down a hallway painted eggshell white with black-framed family portraits arranged at even intervals. Nasim points out each room, opening them to reveal perfectly made beds and watercolors framed on the walls.

"We gave you the largest room," she says. I look at her expectant smile but say nothing. "It used to be my room. I had the servants move all my things to the room next door just a few days before the wedding. I wanted you to have the bigger room with the only private bathroom in the house. I thought it would help you feel more at ease."

I stare at her. What does she want me to say? Do wardens expect gratitude from inmates for the luxuriousness of their cage?

We walk through the family room and living room, each with leather couches and oak coffee tables. Nasim opens two large French doors, leading to an expansive verandah. She points to the wicker furniture and shade trees. "Those trees were pricey, but Amin's father spared no expense."

We walk up to the second floor. "I'm sure it's nothing like what you had back home." She studies my face. "But we have everything we need. The right attitude can make anything good."

As I look out from the balcony, I feel light-headed. The fields behind their house stretch beyond the point of perception, a large expanse of green and brown. Closer to the house, a few goats graze next to a round brick well with a small steeple.

"That well is dry." Nasim nods toward the well. "We have running water in the house, of course. But for mopping or other such things, we use the hand pump." She points to a metal cylinder in the distance. "We have servants for that. You should still learn how to use it, though. Maybe Saba can show you one day when you're not a new bride anymore."

I swallow, turning away from Nasim's gaze, as the curve of her smile disappears.

Chapter 33

I've been here two days. A week and a half to go until I visit my parents.

I step into the bedroom. I don't need a calendar to know that the university orientation has come and gone. I wonder what Carla thought when I never showed up. What did Saif tell her? I draw a sharp intake of breath. *No.* I shake my head. *I can't think about him. I can't.*

Just then, the bedroom door opens. It's Amin.

Now that I'm clear-headed, I see him as if for the first time. He's wearing his work clothes, gray slacks, a crisp white shirt, and a navy blue tie. He's at least six feet tall, with broad shoulders and curly hair. His eyes, with which he looks at me now, are a light shade of brown. In another world, I might even have thought he was handsome.

Since the first night, when he slept on the couch, an uneasy routine has formed. Each night he enters the bedroom. He studies my tense expression. And each night he carefully folds his clothing, places his wallet on the dresser, and throws a pillow on the sofa. I lie in bed, eyes closed but my mind awake, my heart in my throat, wondering what will happen next. So far, nothing has.

This can't last forever, but I don't need it to. I will visit my parents soon. Once I'm at my uncle's house, I'll figure out what to do. I'll talk to Selma. I'll talk to Imran. No matter what, I'm not coming back.

I watch him step into the bathroom. I hear water running. I need to act fast. My only goal is to pretend to be asleep before he steps out of the bathroom. I pull out my earrings and place them on the dresser and slip out of my shoes. I do not hear the bathroom door open. I do not see him step outside. I do not hear him move close to me until he is right behind me.

"Are you okay?"

I turn around and gasp. I take a step back.

Amin's face colors. "I didn't mean to startle you. I just was wondering if you're all right."

"I'm okay."

"You don't seem okay."

"Well, I am."

"You just seem so sad." He runs a hand through his hair. "I know the marriage is new and we don't know each other yet, but you're my wife, and you won't even look me in the face."

Marriage. Wife. This man, with whom I've exchanged no more than two sentences since the day I arrived in this home, dares to call himself my husband? Tears spring fresh to the surface despite my efforts to breathe deeply.

"I'm sorry," he says. "I didn't mean to upset you." He walks up to the nightstand and pulls a tissue. He hands it to me. "I can't believe I made you cry."

We stand in silence for a long minute.

"Florida!" he finally exclaims. I look up at him through my tears.

"Florida?"

"Yes, you're from Florida, right?"

"Yes," I say warily.

"What's it like there?"

I stare at him. First a lecture on being his wife, and now he wants to know about Florida? He walks over to the sofa and sits down.

"They have beaches, right?"

I sit down at the edge of the bed. Small talk. Space, in exchange for conversation.

"Yes." I nod. "There are many beaches."

"Were there any where you lived?" He leans back, his hands in his lap.

"There was one just five miles from our house," I finally reply.

"Did you go often?"

That night, I lie in bed, replaying our conversation. I described to him the sandy beaches of Singer Island and the way the ocean gently lapped onto the beach as seagulls flew overhead. I shook my head in disbelief when he told me he had never seen an ocean in his life. What did this conversation signify? I wonder as I drift to sleep. It doesn't mean what he might want it to mean, but maybe if I go along with this, these simple requests for conversation, he will spare me just a little while longer.

Chapter 34

My sister is coming in a few hours," Nasim says over lunch the next day. "Can you put something decent on before she arrives? There are at least ten outfits pressed and hanging in your closet. It shouldn't be too difficult to pick one." She stops and regards Feiza. "I remember when you first arrived, every day a new outfit and a new gold set. A proper bride."

Feiza fidgets in her chair and casts a glance in my direction. I feel Nasim's eyes on me, but I refuse to look back at her.

"She just has a good attitude," Saba says. "Usman is away more than he is home, thanks to the military always stationing him as far away as they can, but have you ever seen her complain? She has a good temperament. Not everyone is gifted with that."

The chair scrapes as I abruptly get up and make my way to the bedroom and shut the door. I lean against it and take a deep breath.

"Who would have known what a spell she would cast over my brother?" I freeze at the voice bouncing off the tiles. "I told you this match was a mistake, didn't I?"

"Saba." Nasim's voice hardens. "This marriage just may be the best decision I ever made for this family. How else do you think you're getting to America? Your engagement broke three years ago. God knows there isn't any hope for you to marry here. What other chance will you get to start your life over again? I suggest you keep your opinions on my decisions to yourself."

I press my hands to my forehead. *I'm their ticket to America.*

"She's stubborn, but she'll adjust. It's just the other thing. Feiza, stop looking at me like that—we're all women here. I need you to talk to her."

"Ami," I hear Feiza protest, "how can you be sure?"

"I saw with my own eyes. Don't look at me that way! I never meant to spy on them," Nasim snaps. "I just wanted to bring them some breakfast, so I used the spare key to unlock the door and let myself in, and there they are, my son asleep on the old sofa and the new bride sleeping on the bed. I check every day—same thing."

"Why don't you say anything?" asks Saba.

"How can I? I can't bring it up to my son, but something has to be done."

I sink to the floor. A strange emotion passes over me, one I haven't felt in weeks. Not since my chacha snatched me from the bus. But now? Now it feels like pinpricks in my chest. Something has snapped. For the first time in a long time, I am angry.

The doorbell chimes in the distance. I hear laughter. Conversation fills the house. I tie my hair back and turn to the mirror to look at myself in the drab gray outfit before stepping out. Everyone is sitting around a broad-shouldered woman in a green salwar kamiz.

"Ah, the new bride!" she exclaims upon seeing me. She runs her eyes from my head down to my bare feet. Her eyes grow large and then a slow smirk spreads across her face.

"Good choice, Nasim," she tells her sister.

I watch Nasim's face pale as she takes in my cotton salwar kamiz, my unkempt hair, my face devoid of make-up.

I walk back to the bedroom. The door rattles when I slam it shut. This changes nothing, but maybe it sends a message, however small.

"Are you awake?" Amin asks the next morning.

I sit up in the darkened room. He slips on his shoes and ties his black laces.

"I'd rather be home. I hope you know that." He rests his elbows on his knees. "I haven't had a chance to spend much time with you, but hopefully I can make up for that soon." He smiles at me. I try my best to smile back.

Once he's gone, I lie back in bed and close my eyes. A few moments later, I hear the sound of his car as it pulls out of the driveway. Sometimes, in the quiet moments of the morning after Amin is long gone, I stare out the dark curtained window from where I lie in the bed, pretending the sky behind it rises over my own home, over my own bed. Sometimes I can almost believe for a few moments that I imagined all of this and that I am safe from any danger at all.

My thoughts drift to Selma. And then—Saif. I take a deep breath. I can't go there. I just can't. Not yet.

Just then, the bedroom door swings open.

It's Nasim. She storms up to the window and yanks the curtains apart. Harsh daylight streams into the room, invading every corner and crevice.

I struggle to adjust my eyes against the glaring brightness when I realize she is standing over me.

"It is ten o'clock. Everyone in this house gets up well before eight o'clock. What makes you think you are any different? We've played nice with you long enough. You are not a little princess sitting upon your throne. You are not better than us just because you are from America. And you do not get to insult me in front of my sister. It's clear no one taught you how to be a wife. Your husband may have patience for you. Maybe he doesn't understand what he needs to do. But don't worry. I will teach you." She yanks off my sheets. "Get up. You're going to learn how a proper day is supposed to be."

A strange sense of calm fills me. I get out of bed and walk to the bathroom. I've been expecting her veneer to crack. I've been waiting for this moment. How kind could anyone be who participated in my forced marriage? Purchasing me like a piece of fabric at the store?

I stand in front of the sink and lift my white toothbrush. "What are you waiting for?" Nasim snaps. "Put the toothpaste on the toothbrush and brush your teeth."

I stare at the toothpaste. I want to fling it at her. I want to ask her to try to make me do anything, but *what if she won't let me return to see my parents? Then I'll never escape.* I swallow and lift the toothbrush, pressing it against my teeth.

"Now." Nasim folds her arms. "You will go to the closet and pick an outfit to wear. A *proper* outfit, not one of those wrinkled things you can't seem to get enough of. Once you're ready, come outside. I will show you some chores you will be responsible for." She places a hand on her hip and turns to me. "It would be nice if you wore something we gave you. We spent a good deal of money on your clothes."

Was it half as much as you spent on purchasing me? I think.

The servants hover near the kitchen, watching us with amused expressions. Nasim leads me to the outdoor courtyard and instructs me to hang the hand-washed damp clothing in the open air to dry. They stifle laughter later that afternoon when they watch me knead dough and dust frames.

Strangely, these chores are not as bad as I thought they would be. They give me a sense of reprieve from my reality. As I pump water from the outdoor hand pump and polish the tiles, I feel invigorated. My mind, turned off for so long, feels stimulated again.

Nasim, on the other hand, isn't happy with my work. My pots are never scrubbed properly; they drip too much water, are dried too quickly. Still, her words have not affected me save once after dinner.

"You will keep doing these dishes until they are perfect, and you will keep doing them again and again for the rest of your life until you learn how to do it right." Only then did a tear slide down my face.

The thought of having to live here the rest of my life cracked open a part of my heart that can't hide, no matter how hard I try, how desperately I want to leave.

Chapter 35

No one is yet awake when I step into the kitchen today. I open the cabinet by the stove and pull out the bag of flour. Pouring some into a large metal bowl, I glance around. I'm alone. I set down the flour and make my way to the living room and to the telephone resting on the side table. I lift the receiver to my ear and dial the country code and his number. The phone rings, but immediately, the tin voice of an Urdu-speaking operator informs me the line does not have long-distance service. I place the phone back into its cradle. I've opened every drawer and cabinet searching for calling cards. I knew this last-ditch effort would lead to nowhere, and yet I swallow back my disappointment. By now Saif must know I didn't make it to the embassy.

He must know exactly what happened.

I walk back to the kitchen and sprinkle water into the flour and begin kneading the sticky mixture. Saba has a computer. I managed to sneak into her bedroom yesterday, but her password proved impossible to guess. I know I'll be at my uncle's home soon, but it's not coming quickly enough. Just then, Amin walks into the kitchen.

"You woke up early today." He stretches his arms and yawns.

"I'm just getting the flour ready for parathas," I tell him.

He stands straighter. "I'm sorry, Naila. I will talk to her."

"It's okay. It keeps me busy."

"It's not okay. She promised she would back off, but it looks like she hasn't." He moves closer and lowers his voice. "It's not you. She's in a bad mood lately. My brother Usman just got reassigned to the Northwest Frontier for another two years. It's been difficult for her. She'll get better, but I'll tell her again to take it easy."

"Amin." Nasim rushes into the kitchen. She brushes past me. "I thought I heard your voice. You're not leaving yet, are you? I haven't started making breakfast yet."

He smiles at his mother and looks at me. "I'm about to get ready, but I can't stay for breakfast. I'm going to try to get home early so we can go for an outing."

"What a wonderful idea, I've been wanting to—"

"Just me and Naila. How about it, Naila?"

As quickly as Nasim's eyes sparkled a moment earlier,

they extinguish, though her mouth still remains turned up in a smile. "That's an even better idea," she says. "This is the newlywed time, after all; it might do her some good."

I sit in the passenger seat that afternoon and look out the window. Seeing people milling about on the streets, children playing cricket on the grassy fields, hurts. I remember Seema's children playing barefoot in the field across from my uncle's home. Selma, my brother, so many memories linked together, pop out from locked compartments in my mind. I don't want to remember that life continues to move on, that time has not stood still, as it so often feels these days.

The car jerks as it drives over bumpy roads. I close my eyes. My head throbs.

"Here we are." Amin pulls the car onto the side of the road. He points at a stand just ahead. A wiry vendor with a blue hat and faded blue jeans stands next to a white cart. "See the stand over there? It's small and dingy looking, but they have the best kulfi I've ever tasted. I pass it every day when I go to work, and when it's very hot, I stop and buy one. I'd bring you some, but it would melt before I could get it home to you."

He steps out of the car and opens my door.

I step out and follow him. He hands me a kulfi.

I take a bite. "It's good."

"I'm glad you like it." His shoulders relax. "You know, I've wanted to apologize to you." He takes a bite of his kulfi and glances at me. "I know why you are so quiet, so sad."

My heart skips a beat. I look at him.

"You're disappointed," he says. "I know. I wanted to do a proper honeymoon, but I just started this job, and vacation is hard to come by right now. And, well, I know it must get a bit boring day in and day out. We'll go out more. Maybe get some dinner, just you and me. We also need to get you a computer for the house. Saba won't let anyone use hers. I have one at work, so I haven't needed to have one at home, but I know you probably need one."

I stare at him. He continues talking, but I can't seem to focus. The way he looks at me, tries to make me feel comfortable, shows me he has no clue about what I am feeling. He just thinks I'm shy. Homesick. He has no idea what is going on. I hear his voice in the background now, his promise to let me choose our vacation spot, his efforts to come home earlier from now on to spend time with me.

Should I tell him? I wonder. *He would be horrified if he knew the truth. Maybe he'd even help me figure this out.* But no, I know I can't do that. I can't trust what he will do if he finds out about Saif, not when I'm so close to seeing my parents and Selma.

We finish our kulfis and walk back to the car. He tries to meet my gaze, but I'm too busy trying to make sense of this new feeling emerging—not anger but, instead, pity.

He's not a bad man, I think to myself, but his being not bad doesn't mean I want to know him further.

Chapter 36

My hair clings to my neck. Sweat drips down my face as I sweep the verandah under the morning sun. Another blackout has come without warning.

Feiza and Nasim are sitting under a shaded tree in the garden a short distance away. Zaina tosses a green plastic ball to Nasim. I watch Nasim laugh and walk over to Zaina, scooping her up into an embrace, smothering her in kisses. Zaina's squeals of delight peal through the morning air.

I pause to take them all in. Feiza, Nasim, Zaina— they're all . . . happy. Watching them, I remember yet again what an outsider I am here. Maybe this could have been a perfectly nice life for someone.

Just not me.

Right then, Nasim looks at me. Our eyes lock. Her relaxed demeanor evaporates. Standing up, she walks over to me.

"My son is a good man." Her voice shakes. "He has been nothing but the best son any child could ever be. He didn't deserve *this.*" Her cheeks redden. "I don't want to treat you this way, but until you learn to be respectful, until you learn to be a proper *wife*—and you know what I'm talking about." She stares at me. "Things will remain exactly as they are when you return."

I watch her stalk back into the house. Any goodwill I felt toward her fades. *I'm not coming back,* I want to shout. This is the only thought that keeps me going. In two days, I'll be back at my uncle's home. When I go back, I'll find a way out. Selma will get me a calling card. She'll find a way to get me money, to find a different bus. She'll help me think of something. Anything. I don't know how, but I know I'll find a way out. I have to.

I wipe my forehead. I couldn't care less how angry Nasim gets. I am thankful. I've still been spared.

I step into the house; the lights are back on. I take a deep breath of the cool air-conditioned air.

"Can you believe how much time has already passed?" I look up. Feiza is standing by the fridge, watching me tentatively. "We spend our entire lives waiting to get married, and then it just comes and goes in an instant."

I look at my hands, still deep orange with wedding henna.

"Usman, you met him the first time we came to see you at your chacha's home, remember? He had to leave the morning after our wedding. You're lucky that Amin bhai is not going anywhere. I've seen my husband perhaps three full months in our three years of marriage."

"You don't go with him?" I ask her.

"Ah, so you can speak!" She laughs but quickly stops. "I'm only teasing." She glances down the hallway and then lowers her voice. "I wanted to go with him. Usman wanted me to join him as well, but I got pregnant." She blushes. "And they didn't think it was a good idea for me to travel in my condition. I always meant to join him, but somehow I'm still here." She shrugs. "I don't mind so much. It's nice to have help." She pauses. "It's good to accept what is. I try not to dwell on what I don't have. When you get married, things change. I've learned over time to accept this."

Maybe you learned to accept this, I want to tell her. *But I won't ever accept this as my life.* Of course, I say nothing. I bite my tongue and walk away. Soon enough, everyone will know exactly how I feel.

Chapter 37

"*Y*ou don't like the sweets I brought, do you? They're usually a lot better," Amin says to me that evening.

"I do like them." I take another bite of the round yellow ladu. "I'm just stuffed now."

"There's another store, a little farther away. I'll come home early, and we can go there together." He leans in. "And, don't tell anyone yet, but next week? When you get back from your uncle's, we're going somewhere special. It's a surprise, though."

"Amin, I need to talk to you." It's Nasim. She walks up to us with crossed arms.

In an instant, his playful expression is gone. "I'm not in the mood today."

"Amin. It wasn't a question."

I watch him exhale. He turns to me with an apologetic expression before following Nasim to her bedroom. Saba glares at me and pushes her chair back. I watch her stomp away.

These arguments between Nasim and Amin are new. Every night, for the past few days, they stay in her bedroom, exchanging angry words. Each argument ends the same, a loud slam of the door and Amin walking into the bedroom breathing heavily.

Today is no different. I hang my clothes in the armoire. Angry voices vibrate through the wall, but I can't make out the words. I part my hair and braid it, tying the ends with dark rubber bands. Just then, a door slams. The windows rattle; the watercolor paintings tremble.

The bedroom door swings open. Amin's cheeks are flushed. I try to meet his gaze, but he looks away and marches toward the bathroom. I stand frozen until I hear the shower running.

He emerges from the shower several minutes later, a towel around his waist, his hair slick. I take a step back. He seems to hardly notice I'm there. I watch him open the closet by the sofa. He grabs his pajamas and walks back to the bathroom.

I sit down at the edge of the bed. I'm starting to feel unsettled. He's the one who normally tries to make conversation, trying to lighten the mood. I've never seen him this somber before. He steps out of the bathroom now and walks over to the closet. His expression remains grim.

I'm tempted to just turn off the light and go to sleep, but I stand up, making my way toward him.

"Are you okay?" I ask him.

No response. He stands up and pulls a sheet from the closet and tosses it onto the sofa.

Nasim is skilled at twisting words until they cut deep enough to bleed. I can't believe she's doing this to her own son. He's been nothing but kind to me, and now he suffers because of it.

I step closer to him. His back is turned. One hand rests on the top shelf of the closet.

"You can talk to me, you know." I tap his arm. "What's wrong?"

At this, he turns around. I take a step back, not realizing how close I was until just now. Amin moves even closer, filling the empty space between us.

"Naila?" He reaches out and grabs my hand. I flinch. His callused hands feel like needles pricking me, drawing blood. "We're married. We're husband and wife. I want us to be happy, I really do."

I pull my hand from his and draw back.

"I don't understand." He lets out a loud breath. "I've tried really hard to help you feel comfortable, but you just can't stand the sight of me."

"It's not that."

"What is it, then? Please tell me. What can I do to help you be more comfortable here? When will you look at me like a wife is supposed to look at her husband?"

There's nothing you can do. I stare at the floor, unable to meet his gaze.

Sleep eludes me tonight. The way he looked at me, his hand against mine—

Stop it, I tell myself. *He's a good person.* I shift again, pressing the pillow to my body. *He's my friend.* I just need him to be my friend for two nights. Just two more before I can leave.

Chapter 38

My last night. I step into the bedroom and unzip my suitcase, placing my things inside. I glance inside the top drawer of the dresser, filled with jewelry. I pull out the gold and ruby necklace and emerald earrings my mother gave me. I zip up the suitcase and rest it against the wall.

Our conversation from last night rings in my head. "We're husband and wife," he said. His words leave me cold. How can this be a marriage? I am here against my will. He is not my husband. He's someone I must endure. Nasim is not my mother-in-law; she's just a warden. This is not a home. It is a cage.

I realize it is not fair to Amin that he married me, but what about any of this is fair?

I secure the bathroom door before changing. When I step outside, the bedroom is still empty. I turn off the lights and get into bed.

The voices next door are louder tonight. I tense. I can

hear Nasim say in a muffled voice, "Going home . . . not welcome . . . set her straight . . . What kind of marriage . . . drop her back . . . tell her parents . . . keep her . . ."

"You know what would happen if we did that!" he bellows, unequivocally clear.

"I know . . . you two never . . . decide . . . she won't return . . ."

Did I hear her right?

Nasim wants me gone. Nasim wants Amin to drop me off at my uncle's for good. I hadn't imagined this, not even in my wildest fantasies. If Nasim wants me gone, it's as good as done.

I squeeze my hands together. My parents will be angry when I return home like rejected merchandise, but what choice will they have but to take me back? I imagine my mother's lips pressed tightly together. Her eyes wet with tears. My father may never speak to me again, but right now none of this matters. What matters is I can go home!

I settle back into bed when another thought overtakes me. *Set her straight.* What did that mean? I do everything she asks of me. What more can she demand? Suddenly, I freeze. No. I shake my head. His mother is a strong force, but his character is ultimately his own. He would never do that.

When Amin finally comes in, I watch him through half-closed eyes as he goes into the bathroom. He shuffles in the darkened room. I hear him fumble with his sheets and then silence overtakes the room.

Slowly, I allow my body to relax. I lie on my side, one hand under my pillow, sleep finally overtaking me. I think of Saif. I'll see him again soon. I'll wrap my arms around his neck. I'll kiss his lips. Soon I will be safe.

Suddenly, I stir. I feel a strange sensation on my neck, hot and humid. I stiffen.

"Naila?" His voice is low. My pulse quickens. I close my eyes and try to remain still. His warm breath burns my neck. The bed shifts. He's moving closer.

"Naila." He runs a hand through my hair. His fingers trace my jaw, my cheek, my lips.

I gasp as his lips press against my neck. "What are you doing?" My voice is unrecognizable to my ears. Instead of moving away, he edges closer. I try to sit up, to reach for the light on the nightstand, but his hands press against my shoulders, pushing me down. I twist my body, trying to wrench free, but I can't move. I press my hands against his chest, but he seems not to notice. "Please don't," I weep as I beat my hands against him. I can't move. His weight overpowers me. In the dark I can't make out his face, his eyes. He can't see my tears. Who is this person? Where is the man I knew these past few weeks?

I try turning my face from him. I try to stop him from touching me.

"I'm sorry," he whispers. My arms are pinned behind me. My body is racked with sobs as he pulls at my clothing. Screams are useless; they mean nothing in a home of conspirators. "Naila"—his breathing grows more labored—"forgive me."

Suddenly, I scream. Pain envelops me. The world is white, illuminated with pain.

I lie still after, staring up at the ceiling, silent tears falling down my cheek.

"I'm sorry." His voice breaks. "I didn't have a choice."

I press the sheets tightly around myself. I feel numb.

My mind empty but for one thought, one irrational yet clear thought that continues to echo through my mind so forcefully, I fear I might go mad: *Saif. You didn't come in time.*

Chapter 39

*M*y suitcase leans against the wall of the tiled foyer.

Feiza's daughter, Zaina, totters over with careful but clumsy steps. She gazes at my suitcase and then curiously at me before tugging at my kamiz. I look into her wide brown eyes. She giggles and turns around, waddling away with a squeal. I try smiling, but I can't. I am empty.

Footsteps approach. Nasim protests, "Amin, there is no need—you will be late for work. I'll call and get Nuzzhat's driver to take her."

Amin says nothing. He grabs the handle of the suitcase and steps outside.

He opens the back door of the car and places the suitcase inside. Nasim follows me as I step outside. Her usual angry expression is gone. She is smiling.

"We'll see you when you get back, Naila."

The engine hums to life. I look out the window as brick and concrete homes pass by. Dullness cloaks me. All emotions, all energy, vanished for good.

We swerve to avoid a pothole, and I glimpse a young girl of about eight standing on the side of the road, holding a little boy's hand. Dark hair pokes out of her red scarf. I once held my brother's hand. I once led him to kindergarten just as she grips his hand to cross the street. Was that my life once? I wonder. It feels like it was two lifetimes ago.

Amin parks the car on the side of the road by my uncle's home. Turning the engine off, he watches me.

"Naila." He touches my arm.

I wince and pull away. My eyes well with tears.

"Naila." His voice catches in his throat. "I wish I could explain it to you. I had no choice." He pauses. "I am sorry."

Wordlessly, I step out of the car. My uncle locked me in a barred room. My parents drugged me and forced me into this marriage. I didn't think anything could get worse, but today, for the first time, I know what it is like to feel completely broken.

Chapter 40

She's here! She's here!" a voice shouts from a distance. My five-year-old cousin Lubna is running out of the house. She makes her way toward me and hugs me. "I missed you!"

"I missed you too."

Amin carries my suitcase. Aunts and uncles and cousins now stream out of the house to welcome us. Looking out at the faces smiling at me with expressions of love, I feel nauseous.

"Look at you!" Khala Simki's eyes light up as she hugs me. She seems not to notice my hands hanging limp at my sides. "Marriage has done you good. Look how beautiful you are!"

My mother approaches me. Her eyes crease with her smile. "Beta." She reaches out to embrace me, but no—I can't. I take a step back and look away.

She clears her throat. "It's so good to see you again,

Amin." She turns to him. "Thank you," she says, "for letting her stay with me for a little while before we leave."

"Where's Imran?" I ask.

"Oh." My mother adjusts her scarf. "Well, your father and Imran had to leave. Imran had school, and your father had to get back to the store."

"They're gone?" Amin says incredulously. "You should have called us. I could have dropped her off sooner so she could say good-bye."

"It was a last-minute decision," my mother says, "and we didn't want to bother you."

My brother and father are gone.

I try to process this.

They've resumed their life, as though I was never a part of it. I want to feel something, but no emotion rises to the surface. I feel outside of myself, observing events in a parallel universe I no longer inhabit. Conversations swirl around me. Hugs. Smiles. Kisses. They all seep through me completely.

Bilal grabs the suitcase from Amin, while my chacha, who has yet to look in my direction, ushers Amin into the living room. I sit down on the sofa. My mother sits next to me. She grips my hand. I hear the chimes of teacups and look up. It's Selma. She's holding a wooden tray with chai; her eyes are downcast.

Selma, I want to call out to her, *look at me. Are you okay?* I swallow. I know now is not the time.

"We went to Lahore, all of us, three different cars. It was pure chaos." My mother's voice is higher than usual. "I got you a few more outfits. I think you'll like them." She squeezes my limp hand.

Glass plates filled with colorful sweets are placed on the coffee table. I look around the room. There are no remnants of the tears so recently shed in this very home. This is once again a respectable house filled with respectable people. They are now loving relatives welcoming a newly married, dearly missed daughter, back for her brief visit.

I feel sick.

"I have to get to work." Amin stands up.

"Already?" My mother frowns. "We made so much food. We thought you would stay until dinner."

"She's right." Khala Simki emerges from the kitchen. "This is your first time in our house as a married couple. We are making five different dishes and—"

"I'm sorry." Amin walks into the foyer and slips on his shoes.

I stay seated. My relatives hover close by.

"I'll see you later," Amin mumbles as he steps outside.

I don't turn around.

I walk down the hall to the bedroom I inhabited just a few weeks ago. I have just stepped inside when I hear a gentle tap on the door. It's Selma.

"I'm so happy to see you." She plays with the edge of her scarf. "I'm not supposed to talk to you, but how can I do that? I can't not speak to you."

At this my face flushes and my hands involuntarily begin trembling. Selma rushes up to me.

"Sit." She places an arm around me and guides me to the bed. "Are you okay?"

Her warmth unleashes all the pain inside of me. I fear I might never stop crying. Selma says nothing, holding me firmly in her embrace. "I know," she says. "It was never supposed to be this way."

I take a deep breath and try to steady myself. I look at Selma, and for the first time, I really see her. Where did these new circles, dull and dark, under her eyes come from? Why hadn't I noticed them earlier?

"What did they do when they found out you helped me?"

"Nothing happened." She looks at her hands. "I got lucky—nothing happened to me."

"Selma. You're one of the strongest people I've ever met, but you don't have to be strong with me. What did they do?"

"Nothing." She smiles at me, though her eyes are moist now.

I watch my cousin study the edge of her kamiz with careful scrutiny. She's done more for me than I could have ever imagined, and I have no idea what price she paid for it.

I wanted to ask her to help me, but I can't make her pay any more. I take a deep breath and wipe the tears from my eyes. "Let's go outside and see everyone. They'll wonder what we're up to, cooped up in here by ourselves."

"But you just were crying. Something is the matter," Selma begins. "You have to tell me what happened. You know you can still talk to me about anything."

I shake my head and stand up. "Don't worry, I'm fine. I got a little emotional coming back home after all this time. I'm fine."

Chapter 41

"Are you happy, Naila?" my mother asks the next day. We are in the living room surrounded by people. She takes a sip of tea and watches me.

I stare at her. How can she ask me this? As though nothing has happened? My face flushes. I can't speak.

"I'm leaving Tuesday, but you'll be back with us soon enough. I hear they're granting visas faster these days."

Khala Simki leans in. "You know Shamim's son? He got married to an American girl three years ago. Her parents let the bride go back to the US without him!" She raises her eyebrows. "They said he can come when he gets his visa. Three years have gone by, and the girl never even came back! His parents are threatening divorce if she doesn't come back soon."

My mother frowns. "She went back to finish school, didn't she? That's the one, right?"

"Yes. Now, you tell me, what is more important?

Finishing school? Or your marriage? So Naila might miss out on a year or two of college, but priorities are priorities!"

"A year or two?" I look at my mother.

She fidgets and looks into her teacup. "Usually it only takes six months or so, but I think Amin is working on a visa for his mother to come for a little while and to help everyone settle in because his sister will be joining them too. I think the extra paperwork might delay things a little bit, but no more than a year."

I swallow, pushing back the words rising like bile in my throat. *Not now,* I tell myself. I haven't found a way out. Until I do, I can't risk their suspicion.

"In some ways this is a good thing." My mother looks at me. "This way Naila can spend time with her new family. It's good now in the early years to develop an attachment, a bond with his mother and family."

At this, my khala laughs. "So tell me, does a wife ever bond with her husband's mother?" She stops laughing abruptly and looks at my mother, her face reddening.

My mother looks at her sister and shifts in her seat. "That is a problem in our culture." She places her teacup on the side table. "That is why we were interested in Amin's family. His mother is a good woman. She's educated. Those things show. I also watched how she treated her other daughter-in-law. It comforted me. I wouldn't have let you marry just anyone without making sure." My mother searches my face for a response, but despite my greatest effort, I can do nothing but stare at her.

The conversation continues in the main room, but I take my cup to the kitchen and set it down in the sink. Walking down the hallway, I go into my parents' bedroom. I open the drawers in the nightstand, the dresser, the armoire. Maybe my father left my phone behind. Maybe if I look hard enough, I'll find it. I put my hands on my hips and look around the room.

"It's gone."

I freeze. Selma is at the door, watching me.

"What's gone?"

"The phone. Your dad, he destroyed it."

"You're sure?"

"Yes," she says softly. "I saw the broken pieces in the trash can after you got married."

I walk to the window and look outside. The sun is full center in the sky, its blinding heat frying the plants just sprouting from the ground. I grip the edge of the windowsill, but my knees buckle under me. I sink to the floor.

Selma sits next to me and squeezes my hand. After a

few moments of silence, she speaks. "Is he kind to you? He seems kind."

"He's kind." I let out a harsh laugh. "Very kind."

"Does he hit you? Does he yell at you?"

"No," I tell her, "he doesn't."

"Good. This world, it's full of so many bad men. They beat their wives. They scream at them and intimidate them. When I saw him at the wedding, I could tell he looked like a good man. I see the way he looks at you with respect. How many people look at their wives the way he looks at you? I know you didn't want this, but in some ways you are lucky."

"Selma, I don't love him." I turn to her and grip her hands. "I need you to help me. You're the only one who can. Please. I can't go back to that house. I just can't. Do you know where the calling cards are? Your parents must have them still. I know you have already done so much for me, but if you could just get one calling card for me, just one, I'd be forever grateful to you."

"I don't know where they keep them anymore."

"Selma, I know I've gotten you in trouble. I'm so sorry, but please, just tell me where they are. I won't ask you for anything again."

"Why do you want to call him?"

I stare at her. "Why do you think I want to call him? I

haven't spoken to him in weeks. He has no idea what happened. I need to tell him. I can only imagine what's going through his head. He has a right to know. Maybe he could help me—"

"And what good will it do if you call him?" she interrupts. "Is he going to come and take you away from here? He couldn't do it last time."

"Fine." I stand up. "Don't help me. I'll leave on my own. I'll find a way out."

"You're going to try to escape again? Do you know how closely they're watching you? Try stepping into the kitchen for water tonight. Look and see how many people come out to check. Chacha is making Bilal, our servant, sleep on a charpay by the front door the whole time you're here. They're all smiling and acting as if everything is fine, but they're not taking any chances."

"So there must be some other way." My voice wavers. "If we just think hard, we can figure it out."

Selma rubs her temples with her fingers.

"Selma," I plead. "You're like my sister. You've been on my side from the start. Please don't turn your back on me now. I need you."

"I'm not turning my back on you. How could I ever do that? But I'm telling you, there's nothing more to be done. Where are you going to go? Even if you left this house? I have no more money. How far can you get?"

"I can go through the fields." My voice rises. "I'll zigzag through, I'll keep going. I have jewelry. It must be worth something."

"They'll find you. No matter where you go, they'll find you. He can't help you anymore."

"If I could talk to him, he might." My voice breaks into sobs.

"Naila, just think about it for a second. Really think about it. Is this fair to him?"

"To Amin?" I shriek.

"To Saif. Is this fair to Saif?"

"Selma." I stare at her. "Saif loves me. He would do anything for me."

"I know he does, but things have changed. You are not the same person anymore. Honestly ask yourself, is this fair to him? My mother always says when you fight destiny, destiny fights back. Some things, they're just written in the stars. You can try, but you can never escape what's meant to be. You've tried. You both tried very hard to fight your destiny, but things didn't improve—they just kept getting worse. If you really love Saif, stop torturing him. Let him be free to move on. To live his life."

I want to yell at Selma right now, but something about her words settles like ice over my heart. How many sleepless nights have I given Saif? From the start of our relationship, he's had to hide and sneak and change everything about himself. I've given him nothing but paranoia, fear, and now, pain and worry. I'm caught and contained. Am I supposed to drag him along? For how much longer? College classes start next week, but my dreams of college vanished the day I stepped off the plane. Reaching out means asking him to destroy his dreams too. I close my eyes as tears slip down my face.

Selma is right. The harder I struggle, the more painfully destiny pushes down my fate. How long can I push against it? Should love involve pulling the person you claim to love deeper into your own destructive life, to be destroyed along with you? Saif and I tried. We failed.

Only a few months ago, I saw him sitting across from me in the moonlit night in the forest behind my parents' home. I remember resting my head against his chest. I remember the security I felt. I was safe from the world. I close my eyes, longing to find that feeling again, but instead all I find is emptiness. I can never fill this void. Selma is right. The girl Saif loved is dead. Some things, once lost, are irretrievably gone.

Chapter 42

It takes me most of the night to write it. But finally, the letter is complete. I seal the worn envelope I found tucked in Selma's drawer. This envelope once held the money with which I tried to escape. Now it seals my fate. I write Saif's name and the address of our old high school on the letter. Eventually it will make its way to him. Eventually he'll know what happened and will be able to put this part of his life behind him.

The sky is getting brighter; light shines through the barred window. I look over at Selma, who is rousing from sleep. I get up and walk over to her.

"What is this?" asks Selma, looking at the paper in my hands. She rubs her eyes and sits up.

"It's the last favor I'll ask of you." I wipe away a tear. "You were right. I can't do this to him. But I have to let him know. I can't let him wonder. It will only hurt him more. Please send this for me. I won't ask you for anything else."

Selma takes the envelope and looks at me, her eyes watering. "I never wanted this for you."

"I know." I look away. "But this is my life now. It's time I accept it."

That afternoon, at a quarter to twelve, there is a knock on the door.

My chachi frowns. Bilal opens the door. It's Amin.

"Amin." My mother stands up. "What a surprise! Come in. We are just about to eat lunch."

"We need to go. I came to take Naila back," Amin responds from the doorway.

"What do you mean?" My mother walks up to him. "My flight is tomorrow."

Amin looks at me.

"Is it okay if we leave?" he asks.

"Yes," I reply.

Chachi walks into the foyer. "Is everything okay? Your mother is well?"

"She's fine."

"At least stay for lunch, then?" My mother's voice wavers. "Or chai? I can start boiling the water. It will only delay you a few minutes."

"I'm sorry."

My mother stares at him.

A tense silence settles over the room. Bilal brings my small black suitcase and hands it to Amin. I walk past my mother toward the front door.

The brightness of the sun reflects off the metal exterior of his car.

"Wait!" my mother calls out. She walks up to us.

"I'll call you when I land," she says. Tears flow down her face now. Her cheeks are flushed. She hugs me tightly. "I love you."

I open the car door.

"No good-bye?"

I've avoided saying anything to her since I came back yesterday. I've stayed quiet. But I think of Saif, of everything I lost, and suddenly my anger is a sensation so hot, I can taste it. It burns on my tongue.

"Good-bye?" I repeat. I stare at her. "All my life, I did everything I could to be a good daughter. I followed all the rules. I did everything to make you proud of me, and for what? You sold me off. You threw me away like a dirty towel you didn't want anymore, and now? Now, you want heartfelt good-byes from me?"

"Naila." My chacha lowers his voice and presses a hand on my shoulder. "This isn't the time or the place—"

"No!" I shove his hand off of me. My voice breaks. A tear slips down my face. "You don't get to tell me the time or place for anything anymore." I look at my relatives. Their arms are crossed. They wear frozen smiles on their faces. Amin is sitting in the running car. I don't know if anyone can hear me, but I no longer care.

"You're my daughter. My only one." My mother's voice breaks into sobs. "We did what we did for you."

"I *was* your daughter. I'm not anymore."

I feel my mother's gaze on me as the car pulls away.

I never want to look at her again.

Chapter 43

*T*he car ride home is silent. The servants open the steel gates, and Amin pulls into the carport. Nasim and Saba walk outside, shielding their eyes from the sun. They watch us approach.

"Welcome home." Nasim hugs me. "Ruqaya, my dear friend, stopped by for some chai. I didn't realize you'd be home so soon. Come in and meet her."

I step into the foyer.

"There she is!" I look up and see Ruqaya. Short and perfectly round, she wears a bright yellow salwar kamiz and smiles at me widely before she clears her throat and then, slowly, in broken English says, "It is nice . . . to meet you."

I swallow and look back at her.

"That bad?" She laughs, switching back to Urdu. "Well, maybe now that you're here, you can teach me how to speak it properly."

I look down at the ground. Just days earlier, I thought I would never have to set foot in here again.

"I'm making some tea." Nasim takes my hand and leads me toward the kitchen. "Just help me set out the biscuits, and you can teach Ruqaya all the English she wants."

"We need some time alone," Amin says.

"First, some tea." Nasim looks at Amin with surprise. "And then you can have as much alone time as you want."

"It can't wait."

Nasim releases her grip. "Fine. I'm starting the tea— don't be long."

I follow him toward the bedroom. I watch him lock the door. My heart races. *My knee,* I think. *If he dares try . . .*

"Have a seat." He points to the worn sofa but catches my expression. His voice falters. "I mean, only if you want to."

It's been only a few days, but I'm shocked at the depth of betrayal I feel. I had no right to expect anything from him. Still, the humiliation stings.

Amin paces the length of the room, his jaw tense and angular. "First, I'm sorry." He stops and looks at me. His eyes redden. "No, sorry doesn't begin to cover it. I had no right. I have no excuse. I don't expect you to ever forgive me."

He sits down on the bed across from me. "Since you left, I'm haunted with one question. I keep thinking, why does my wife look at me like she does? Why do I have to work so hard to bring one smile to her face? What did I do wrong?"

I watch him rub his temples with his fingers. His tone is heavier than I've ever heard it before.

"I remember when I first saw you. You were wearing a lavender salwar kamiz. You were so different from any other girl I ever met. I must have met twenty others before you, but you know what made me certain I wanted to marry you? It was when we first met and you looked up at me while serving tea and you smiled. Most girls look away, but you looked me directly in the eyes. I thought in that moment we shared some sort of connection. But since then I've never seen a smile like that again on your face. And I have been driving myself crazy in all these weeks trying to figure out what happened, what changed to take away your smile."

I stare at him, trying to recall the moment he remembers as vividly as I don't.

"Then I thought, maybe it's because I can't provide her with the lifestyle she is used to. She is from America, and life is very different there. But the more I thought about it, the way your father just left, the way you looked at your mother. Something didn't make sense." He looks at me. "Then it hit me last night. I realized what it was. You didn't want this, did you?"

I look at him.

"That's what I thought." His face clouds over. "I'm the man they made you marry." He is silent for a few moments. "Why?" he finally asks. "Why did they do it? Was there someone else? Is that why you didn't want to marry me?"

"Amin," I blurt out, "it's *because* there was someone else that all of this ever happened. None of this was my choice." I press a hand against my mouth, trying to regain composure. "His name is Saif." I squeeze my eyes shut, but tears trail down my cheeks.

Amin swallows. "Oh," he says. "I see . . . I had no idea." His voice trails off. "They forced you to marry me."

I look down, unable to speak.

"Do you want to leave?" His eyes are now downcast.

Is this a trick? I wonder. *Does yes mean he will unlock the keys to my cage? Or is he trying to gauge my risk of flight?*

I hold my breath and then, "Yes," I say, looking at him. "I want to leave."

Amin swallows. "I wish life were that simple. I wish I could tell you to just go. But I can't tell you that. Maybe

I could have five years ago, when I was younger and knew less about the way the world works. But one thing I have learned in this life is that you have no control over it. Life chooses us. We think we can control it, but we can't."

"There are some things we can control. You can change this. You can."

"Change what?" he asks. "Change the fact that your uncle will probably kill you if I send you back?"

"Kill me?" I repeat. "Look, Amin, I know he has a temper but—"

"It's more than a temper, Naila."

"It doesn't matter. He knows my father would never let that happen."

"The same father who did this to you?" he asks. "Besides, we can control many things. But not whom we marry. Our marriage was written before we ever existed. We could no more keep this marriage from taking place than we could control the weather." He looks at me. "If you think I want this, I don't. How can I be happy when my wife finds me repulsive? When she will never trust me again? But what can I do? Not only would your life be in danger, we would bring shame to both our families. The little chance my sister has of getting married would be gone." He shakes his head. "I wish I had known all this before we ever got married. I was deceived—my whole family was. Just like you, I feel cheated. But it's too late now. We cannot escape our destiny. There's nothing you can do. There's nothing I can do."

As I watch him get up and walk away, every ounce of hope—the hope I didn't know until now I had bottled up and stored away—shatters, vanishing into the air. My prior life is now better left as a figment of my imagination, a reality wrenched away for good.

Part Three

Chapter 44

"Your face is a window to your world," Saif once teased me as he sat across from me in the high school courtyard. He had pushed his tall red energy drink toward me, insisting I try some, and burst out laughing at my concerted effort to smile as I took a sip.

"It's good!" I had protested with a wince before grabbing and downing my water bottle in one long gulp.

"Don't ever play poker with me." He grinned. "You couldn't lie if your life depended on it."

He was wrong.

The sun has long since set; dinner was over hours ago. I sit on a plump leather couch in the living room of Amin's home. Feiza sits next to me watching television. She hardly blinks. Nasim sits on a recliner across from us hemming Amin's pants. On the surface, everything is exactly as it has been these past three months.

I stare at the television, but nothing registers except the desire to keep my breathing steady and my face as expressionless as possible. No one must know what I am feeling right now. No one can know what happened today.

The morning began like all the others before it. I propped a squirming, giggling Zaina on the kitchen table.

"Zaina!" I lifted up her sandals. "I can't put your shoes on if you keep moving around!"

Feiza walked into the kitchen and shook her head at her daughter. She wrapped a gray chador around her shoulders. "Be a good girl, Zaina, or we won't take you to the market! I mean it this time!"

I love going to the market with Feiza. She picks the things we need while I look after Zaina. Our time there is nothing special, but trips to the market are a chance to escape the four walls of the house, a momentary reprieve from the boredom that otherwise pervades my existence. Now that I've become a permanent fixture, the servants have slowly intervened in my chores, gently insisting I leave the labor to them. They can't understand that I want to clean and dust. I want to scrub the grout until it gleams white. What would I do if I stopped and stayed completely still? I can't be sure, but I fear I might slowly go insane.

Now as I sit on the couch this evening, I think back to what happened and wonder: *Despite my greatest efforts, have I finally gone mad?*

We made our way down the road toward the market as

we did nearly every other day. I remember my shock when I first encountered open-air markets such as these, with raw slabs of red meat hanging on hooks in the open air. Carrots, radishes, and turnips in crates lining the front of the store. It all felt bewildering, but now, a few months later, I can hardly believe I ever shopped anywhere else. Crisp, cool stores with sliding doors and fluorescent lights and stock boys in white aprons talking on cell phones as they line up groceries on white metal shelves now feel like a fable, a fairy tale I might have heard a lifetime ago. This market, the dusty floor, the women's voices at a steady hum, the flies buzzing overhead, this is reality.

I never thought I could feel this way, but it turned out Selma was right: letting go helped ease my anger at the unfairness of it all. I couldn't say I was happy now, but I had accepted that this was my life. The farther away I let the past feel, the more I could accept my reality.

This morning, Bibi Fatima had nodded at us from where she sat by her house on the corner near the market, sorting through her lentils. She smiled a toothless grin at Zaina, as she always did. The market was busier than usual. I recognized most of the women here by their chadors, each with uniquely patterned reds, pastels, and blacks; some women covered their heads with them, others wrapped their chadors around their shoulders. A tall man with a wiry build and thick mustache carefully inspected a fresh batch of goat meat swaying on a hook.

I stood apart from the shoppers as I normally did. Zaina, now more confident in the use of her sturdy legs, no longer let me hold her in my arms. Now she demanded to explore every corner of the store and taste as many things as possible before I inevitably caught her. Today was no different. She whimpered in my embrace, squirming against my hip and pointing toward the floor.

"Okay," I finally told her. "I'll let you walk with me, but hold my hand and don't let go."

I set her on the floor, gripping her hand tightly in my own. She looked up with pleading eyes, her hand tugging mine, small tears forming as she babbled in a language known only to her. I looked at the splotches of red appearing on her cheeks, a tantrum approaching.

"Zaina." I leaned down and kissed her cheeks. "You like sugar cookies, don't you? The ones with the sprinkles? Or maybe some ice cream? You want to go with me to get some?"

I was looking up at the cooling display shelf tucked in the back corner of the store when I suddenly stiffened.

Someone was watching me. I could feel the gaze boring into the side of my face.

I had grown accustomed to the penetrating stares of strange men. Oftentimes the glances were merely curious ones by those passing by and wondering who I was, the one with a gait distinct from the other women in the area. Sometimes, however, my eyes had met those of an admirer, taking me in, seeming to undress me with his gaze. At first, in my anger, I stared back at these men brazenly, expecting them to blush with shame and look away. But I was always the one who ultimately looked the other way; the men seldom did. I grew to understand why Feiza and the other women chose to cover themselves in large chadors, cloaking themselves when out and about, and soon learned to keep my focus on the ground, a charcoal-gray chador cloaking me as well.

Then why now, after months of averting my eyes, had I looked back?

I fidget now on the sofa, trying to keep my eyes fixed on the television. *Why today had I met this gaze?*

I ignored it at first; I did my best to look away. I rushed to catch Zaina, who had yanked her hand from me and raced toward the shelf full of glass spice jars. I scooped her up into my arms. I lifted my hand to adjust my shawl.

And that's when it happened.

I caught for an instant the eyes of a man staring back at me.

It was a strange sight—a figment so real, I could reach out and touch it. Despite the months of perfecting the art of looking away, I was transfixed in shock. Zaina wriggled from my grasp and bounded toward the chickens in the wire coop in the distance, but I could only stare at the hallucination, the strange incarnation standing in the store, a short distance from me.

Saif.

I slowly stood up straight, afraid to move too suddenly, afraid the mirage would vanish. I looked at the cream-colored round hat on his head, his white salwar kamiz, and the light brown chador draped loosely around his shoulders. It wasn't Saif. It couldn't be. This person had light stubble around his jaw. This person had closely cropped hair. Saif in his jeans and wavy hair looked nothing like this person standing across from me, staring at me now.

But why, then, did I see his eyes and recognize some-body familiar?

I felt a tug on my salwar. Zaina held a half-eaten apple. "Up!" she squealed. I reached down and lifted her in my arms. She rested her head on my shoulder, humming softly to herself.

I turned back, but he was gone. Nothing stood in the space he occupied just moments before.

Now, as I stare at the television screen, I wonder, *Is my mind finally cracking?* Why now? After all these months, after I have finally accepted it, why does he haunt me in the faces of strange men in the marketplace?

"Feiza, come with me to the market," I say the next morning.

"We just went yesterday. Did we forget something?" Feiza steps into the kitchen.

"We didn't forget anything—rice wasn't on our list." I pull out an empty sack of rice.

Feiza stares at the empty bag of rice and places a hand over her mouth. "Thank God you checked! What if Saba had noticed first? I swear that bag was nearly full when I checked yesterday." She frowns. "Usman is coming in a few weeks. I'm just too distracted to function properly these days."

I blush, feeling guilty about the upturned rice at the bottom of the garbage can. "I don't know, but we should get some more."

"Give me a minute. Zaina is asleep. I don't want to wake her. Let me make sure Saba can watch her before we go."

I just want to be sure, I tell myself. *I just want to confirm that I simply hallucinated.*

We step into the market and make our way toward the large brown rice sacks at the far corner of the store. "These are going to be heavy." Feiza lifts the handle of the largest bag. "We should have sent Mushtaq. We just got so nervous, we headed over here without thinking. He always brings the rice."

"Let's just pick up a small bag. If we go back empty-handed, Saba will be upset."

Feiza lifts the handle of the smallest bag. "I understand why she's bitter, but we're not the reason her engagement broke. You know she taught at the primary school here before her engagement ended? Nasim still tries to persuade her to go back, but she'd rather sulk at home all day. I wish she would stop taking it out on us."

"Should we tell her that when we get home?"

"You're terrible! Let's go pay for this."

"Let me get some cookies," I tell her. "I promised Zaina I would get her some sugar cookies yesterday, and I forgot."

"You are so good to her." She smiles. "She's lucky to have you."

I watch her make her way to the vendor at the front of the store. She pauses at the stall of fresh produce. I glance around. A handful of women are milling about in the distance. No figments linger in the open-air market today.

I count out the money I brought with me and make my way to the row lined with packaged goods and biscuits. Suddenly, I gasp.

There it is. The hallucination. The same clothing. The same hat. The same stubble. And the same eyes. He's at the edge of the aisle close to me. Close enough to touch. He does not look away. He's watching me.

"Are you okay?"

I turn around. It's Feiza, standing right behind me. "Naila"—she puts a hand on my shoulder—"you don't look well."

"I'm fine." I take a deep breath. "I'm just going to step outside."

"Sure." She watches me with concern. "I'll be just a second."

The world seems uneven, moving faster than it should as I go. Hallucinations are supposed to be blurred, hazy, and translucent. Yet this one seems real. Solid.

The sky grows overcast, giving me reprieve from the otherwise bright sun. The months have passed; the heat has grown more forgiving, and yet—it lingers.

Maybe that's what's going on. I have heatstroke.

I draw in a deep breath and adjust my chador to keep it from sliding down my hair. *A figment,* I tell myself. *You're having some sort of setback. Just take a deep breath. It will pass.*

I am turning back to see if Feiza is nearly done when my heart drops. The figment has stepped outside. He looks at me. He hesitates for a moment. And then he walks toward me.

"Naila," Feiza calls, "feeling any better?" She appears before me, holding the plastic grip of the small rice bag.

I look past her shoulder. He's still there. So close. But Feiza is walking now. Her footsteps leading home. I force myself to follow her, but it's difficult. My legs are made of bricks.

This is no hallucination. It's Saif. Saif is here.

Chapter 45

I sit at the dinner table and stare at my cold plate of food. My hands grip the metal glass of water by my side.

"What's the matter?"

I look up. Nasim is staring at me.

"We're almost done eating, and you haven't even touched your roti."

What can I say? That Saif is here? That he has light stubble and wears clothing I've never seen him in before? But that his eyes still look back at me in the same way they always have? And for this very simple reason, today, right now, I find myself unable to eat?

"Sorry. I'm just not feeling well." Pushing my chair back, I get up. "I think I'm going to lie down."

"She wasn't feeling very good today when we went to the market either," Feiza says as I walk to the bedroom. "I hope she's not coming down with something."

"God forbid the princess should catch a cold!"

"That's enough, Saba," Amin chides his sister as he so often, uselessly, does.

I toss and turn in bed that night. I can't sleep.

Getting up, I slip on my sandals and walk into the family room. I unlatch the hook to the French doors and step outside, taking a seat on a wicker sofa in the courtyard. The darkness cloaks me, and for a moment, I feel invisible. I take a deep breath and release it slowly.

After all this time, how did he find me? I think of the letter I wrote him months ago. I told him to let me go. I told him I had made my peace. I told him to move on. I kept my letter as simple as possible, hoping that by writing it I was releasing him from the burden of hanging on to me. If I couldn't be free, I wanted him to be. It was one of the most painful things I had done.

And yet, despite that letter, how many times had I dreamt in my darkened room that somehow Saif would find me? Every day I had looked for his face in every face I saw. But this hope has long since been extinguished. I was the one who told him to move on. And after three long months of silence, I thought he had.

I look up. The moon is absent, but the stars—for a moment, I am breathless. There are so many stars scattered across the sky tonight, they threaten to overtake the darkness.

I imagine Amin in the bedroom inside, an arm covering his eyes as it normally does, small snores escaping his mouth, completely unaware. I never imagined I would ever speak to Amin again, much less feel anything other than dark hatred, but as time has passed, I've grown tired of the vitriolic emotion bottled inside. I want to hate him, but hating is an emotion that requires more energy than I can muster these days. This wasn't a choice either of us made, and while I don't love him, I thought I had made my peace.

But Saif is here. And now I feel nothing close to peace.

Chapter 46

*I*t's been three days—the longest three days of my life—but it's finally time to go to the market again. I pause and take in the person staring back at me in the bathroom mirror. Circles outline my eyes like charcoal etchings. My mouth is sandpaper dry. I'm trying to seem calm and collected, but I can't eat. I can't drink. Every time reality seems to settle in, every time I think I can begin to make sense of it, I fall into a tailspin once more.

I need to see him.

I take a deep breath and cradle Zaina on my hip. In my tightly clenched fist I hold the message I've written for Saif, hastily scrawled on a scrap sheet of paper.

The road kicks up more dust than usual today. I shield my eyes with one hand to protect against the haze of clay-colored earth. Feiza makes small talk on our way to the market. I try to respond, to appear interested, but I can't focus. As soon as we enter the store, my eyes dart to the shelves, the corners of the walls.

I set Zaina down on the ground. Before I can grip her wrist, she runs toward the spice aisle.

"Zaina!" I make my way toward her. She's hunched over the bottles of pickled mangoes on the bottom row. I grasp her hand and stand up. When I do, I gasp. It's him.

How long has he been standing there? Saif, in a khaki salwar kamiz, at the edge of the aisle, his hand leaning on the shelf, his eyes focused directly on me. Our eyes meet. He is standing so close to me.

He picks up a bottle of crushed chili and examines it.

"Naila." His voice is soft, barely audible. He turns the bottle in his hand, examining it as though it were gold.

I bite my lip. The world grows hazy. My head throbs. My stomach hurts. Saif stands mere inches from me. In an instant, I feel transported. It's as though it's the two of us again. *I want to touch him. Just his arm. Just to make sure he's real.* I tremble and take a step toward him.

Just then, a tug. I look down—it's Zaina, pulling on my kamiz. Feiza is in the distance, coming toward us. I look at Saif and begin panicking. *Has she seen us? Does she know?* I hesitate. My resolve wavers, and yet *if not now, when?*

I push out any other thoughts and walk toward him. His eyes widen, but I avert my gaze. With a sharp intake of breath, I press my hand—and the note—into his. For a fraction of a second, his hand curves over mine.

I step into the open air. Beads of sweat dot my fore-head. I close my eyes and will my hands to stop trem-bling. When I look back, he's gone.

"Who was that?" It's Feiza.

"Who?"

"That man. Did you see him? He's a bit young. I've never seen him here before."

"I didn't see anyone new."

"Probably someone's relative visiting from America. You can always tell by the way they walk that they're not from here."

"Maybe." I bite my lip and do my best to keep my gait steady. Feiza is talking, but all I can think about is the warm touch of his hand against mine. The softness with which he spoke my name. After all these months, despite everything that has happened and how different he looked, he was still Saif. The boy I fell in love with.

And he came all this way for me.

Each step I take away from him feels painful.

Each step away makes me ache for the life I almost had. For everything that was ever home to me.

Chapter 47

*B*y the well behind the house. Tonight.

By now he's read the note. Is he there right now? I look out the window. The sun set hours ago, darkness stretching as far as I can see.

"What is the matter with you?"

I turn around. It's Nasim. She's sitting in the living room. The television is on at full volume, but she's watching me, her arms crossed.

"You've been staring out that window for the past ten minutes."

I turn to her. "Sorry, I just got lost in thought."

Amin is reading a newspaper on the love seat. His eyebrows furrow in concentration. I sit down next to him.

Why won't anyone go to sleep tonight? I look up at the wall clock. It's only nine o'clock. Why does it feel like midnight?

"I forgot to tell you"—Nasim's eyes return to the

bright screen—"your mother called for you while you were in the shower. She said she will try again tomorrow afternoon."

I swallow and nod, but say nothing.

"She called every day this week," Amin says quietly.

"I can't talk to any of them."

"You can't shut them out forever."

"I'll try my best to."

"I know they've betrayed you." He glances around and lowers his voice more. "But they're your parents—they love you. I picked up the phone yesterday, and, Naila, I can hear the pain in her voice when I make excuses for why you can't answer the phone. They know you're avoiding them."

Good, I say to myself.

"My mother asked me today if something happened. She's going to figure out pretty soon why you're in the bathroom, or doing something outside, and unavailable, whenever the phone rings."

"You want me to talk to them and pretend I am okay with everything? I can't do that, Amin."

"I'm upset with them too. But at the end of the day, you only get the two parents you're given. I already lost one, and I can tell you once they are gone, it's too late for regrets."

"I'll think about it."

"What are you two gossiping about?" I look up. Saba is staring at us from across the room.

"It's between us," Amin says calmly. He turns back to me. "By the way, are you sure you don't want to come along with me on the business trip? I could see if I could book you a seat."

"Oh, that." I turn to look at him. I had forgotten all about his trip. "You leave tomorrow?"

"It's all expenses paid. You've never been to Karachi— might be a fun few days."

"You'll be busy with meetings." I force a smile. "I don't want to wander the city alone."

"Well, we need a vacation. When I get back, we'll plan one. Anywhere you want."

He describes mountainside villas and sunny resorts, but all I can think of is the darkness outside. Saif is there.

"I'll be right back." I get up.

Amin looks at me. "Are you okay?"

"I'm fine, I just need a drink of water."

Instead of the kitchen, I make my way to the bedroom. I know I need to play it cool, but each passing minute feels like ten. I need to splash water on my face. Take a few deep breaths. Or else they will not just have suspicions, but certainty, that something is up.

I shut the door behind me. Immediately there is a knock.

Feiza. She pokes her head in. "Can we go a little earlier tomorrow?"

"Where?"

"The market. I heard they're getting a new shipment of produce."

"Sure." I look down at my hands. "That's fine."

"Are you okay?" Feiza asks. "Your face is flushed." She walks over and presses her hand against my forehead. "No fever. That's strange."

"I know." I walk over to the sofa and sit down. "No fever. I just don't feel well."

A look of worry shadows her face. "You've been looking unwell for some time now," she murmurs. Suddenly her eyes light up. "Oh! I understand!"

My heart skips a beat. "What do you understand?"

"You've been in your bed more than I've ever seen you. You threw up yesterday, didn't you? I noticed how you ran out of the kitchen so suddenly. I remember when I began feeling sick for no good reason!"

I frown at her excitement until I realize what she means. "No," I tell her. "That's not it. I think it's the heat. It affects everyone."

Feiza places a hand on my shoulder. "It's hard to know

when you've never felt it before, but I have a good feeling about this. Get some rest. I'll go to the market myself." She pats my hand and leaves the bedroom.

I keep my face frozen in a neutral expression until Feiza leaves. As soon as she's gone, I jump up and lock the door tightly. My face flushes. I've pushed it far from my mind and most of the time I can even pretend it's not real, but Feiza's words bring my reality back into sharp focus.

My hands tremble as I walk into the bathroom.

I knew within a few weeks after returning to Amin's house that something was different. I tried denying it, I made excuses for my growing fatigue, my delayed period. But when the first wave of nausea overtook me shortly after, I could deny it no more. I'm pregnant.

Save the one night I try my best to forget, Amin has not touched me. He understands that while I may go along with this marriage, I will do nothing more. To his credit, he has never mentioned the possibility of doing otherwise. But now, though he doesn't know it, whether I want it or not, he has linked my fate to his for life.

I turn the faucet on and cup my hands under the cold water before splashing it on my face. I've been so careful. I force myself to get out of bed. I pretend to enjoy the food Nasim makes each morning. I even made sure to turn on the shower and faucets when I had to throw up, hoping no one would hear. All so no one would question, no one would suspect.

I press a hand against my stomach—still flat, not revealing a hint of what now lies inside. If I've accepted my place here, there's no reason to keep it a secret—but each time I've tried to say something, the words won't come. Maybe I'm hoping if I can just keep pretending it's not happening, if I just don't say it out loud, somehow it won't be real.

I pace the room. I have found ways to make life bearable the past few months. Like sitting on the balcony on cool afternoons when the clouds hide the sun, watching the horizon expand before me, or at night, trying to decipher the stars that fill up the sky. Amin brings American movies home for us to watch, or we watch Indian ones that are slowly growing on me with their fantasies of singing in gardens and bathing in waterfalls.

I thought I had accepted it all.

I look outside at the oppressive darkness. My chest hurts. I need to see Saif. I need to hear his voice. Talk to him. Just for a little while. I swallow. And then, I have to tell him how different things now are. How they can never be the same again.

It is eleven o'clock. Saba lets out a yawn.

"Are you coming to bed?" Amin asks. He stands up and rubs his eyes.

"I'll be there soon," I tell him. I watch him go to the bedroom.

An hour later, I am alone. I listen for a moment—silence.

I walk to the door leading to the verandah. I take a deep breath and turn off the lights. I press gently until the door parts, then close it soundlessly behind me. The cloudy night obscures all the stars tonight. Aside from the rustle of leaves in the breeze, I hear nothing but silence.

Reaching out my hands, I walk, feeling for the well until my fingers finally press against the cool touch of brick. I brush my hand against its rough exterior and look back at the house. It's disappeared into the darkness on this moonless night.

Just then, I hear a movement and step back. There's someone on the other side of the well, standing just across from me.

I can't breathe.

"Is it you?" His voice is soft and hesitant. "Naila." He walks toward me.

In the silent darkness, without the hustle-bustle of the market, the crying toddler in my arms, with nothing to distract me, the full reality of the situation hits me. This nonhallucination, this real, concrete human being is Saif.

I place a hand on the well. He is so close to me now I can make out the contour of his jaw, the bridge of his nose.

"Saif, what are you doing here?" The English words feel foreign to my tongue.

He touches my hand. I flinch, pulling my hands away. No. I can't let him touch me. If hearing him say my name hurts this much, I won't survive the aftermath of his touch. I might never be able to let go.

"I can't believe this." His voice sounds hoarse. "I can't believe you're here." He moves closer. "Naila, what's the matter? Why won't you look at me?"

All day I thought of what I'd say to him when I finally saw him. I rehearsed every point I would bring up. I promised myself to be strong, to speak gently but firmly, to thank him for coming, and to let him know that he needed to go home because it was now too late. But standing in front of him, I realize the prepared speech is impossible. No matter what has happened in the past few months, this is still Saif. I never could lie to him. It's useless now to try.

"I don't know what to say," I finally tell him. "I can't believe you're here. I can't put into words what it means to me that you came . . ." Struggling, I continue, "The short version is, I tried to escape, but they found me. It was awful, but it's better now. I mean, I'm trying to accept it. I'm trying to make my peace with it." My voice breaks. "Saif, you shouldn't be here. If anyone finds out why you're here, you won't be safe."

"What are you talking about, Naila? This isn't your life. It's over now. You don't have to make your peace with anything."

"No. I have accepted this. I didn't at first. I hated it here. I prayed every day . . . every day I prayed that you would find me." I brush away hot tears welling in my eyes.

"Naila, please listen to me. I tried so hard to find you. I didn't know where you were. I didn't for one minute ever forget you."

I shake my head and press a hand on the rough exterior of the well to steady myself.

"I tried to do everything I could think of," he says. "I called the embassy every day. I begged them to look for you. But for the longest time, I didn't know where you were. I knew you were close to Lahore, but I had no idea which town. I had no idea there were so many towns! I drove to your parents' house every day. I waited for them to come back. I went to them, Naila, your parents. I knocked on your door." He laughs bitterly. "Remember how you used to say it would be so intimidating to meet them? Remember I said I'd win them over with a smile?

"I begged them. I begged them to tell me where you were. I sat on your front porch step and I told them I wouldn't leave until they told me. They stopped opening the door. Forgive me, Naila, but I yelled at your parents. I banged on their door in the middle of the night. I yelled at them for what they did to you." His voice broke. "I did everything I could—they wouldn't help me."

"Good. I'm glad you yelled at them," I say quietly. "Maybe it reminded them they had a daughter."

This time I don't object as he slips his hand into mine. "When I got your letter, I thought, What is this? That's not you. This isn't Naila. These aren't her words. She doesn't talk like this! I didn't care what that letter said. You had to know me enough to know I wouldn't listen to what you said in it.

"Your brother finally helped me. He slipped out a window and told me to meet him in the woods one evening. He told me everything. You know he still feels guilty? As if all of this is his fault. He promised to help me. He finally found your address hidden in a notebook in a drawer in their bedroom. As soon I had that, I came."

"How?" I ask him. "How could you get here all by yourself?"

"My father is here too. He booked our flight as soon as I had an address. We met with the numberdaar of the village next to this town. We've been paying him to stay at his place. It took a month. But I finally found you."

I press my back against the wall and close my eyes. I want the pain to stop. The dark, empty well behind me suddenly feels inviting, enticing. I wish to simply stand at its precipice, to close my eyes, dive in, and escape the pain of the moment I fear will never subside.

He tried. Even when I gave up, he never stopped trying. And yet, he failed. I want to rest my head on his shoulders. I want him to wrap his chador around me. Every atom of my being wills me to meld into him and never let go.

"Naila"—his voice wavers—"what is it? You don't want to stay here, do you?"

"It's not that." I shake my head. "It's just not that simple."

"Why not? I'm here. We can leave now. Why does it have to be any more complicated than that?"

"There are risks."

"I knew there were going to be risks when I came. Those are just risks we'll have to take."

"There's more." I don't know how to tell him, but I do know I want to remember how he looks at me right now so I can have it to remember later, when he might not be able to look at me in the same way.

"Listen." He fidgets and clears his throat. "If things have changed for you—if your feelings about me aren't the same, that's still not a reason to stay."

"My feelings?" I stare at him. "How could you even think that? I love you. I always have. It's just—"

Suddenly, he leans down; his lips press against mine.

Pull away.

But no part of me knows how. After all these months, he's still Saif. I run my fingers through his hair, trace the outline of his face—

And then I kiss him back.

For the first time since I arrived in this house, since I accepted I had no choice but to accept, I finally let myself cry. He wraps his arms around me. I lean my head against his chest. Something shifts inside me.

I can't do this anymore.

Even if Saif can't bear the burden of what I must tell him. Even if it changes everything between us. Even if it's dangerous to leave, I have to. For me. For this child.

And yet, I don't know how to tell him. I don't want to tell him.

"Saif, I'm pregnant."

He pulls away for a moment. My heart drops. I knew this would be too much to handle. He never signed up for any of this. But just then his arms encircle me, and he pulls me close to him.

"Did you hear me?" I whisper. "I'm pregnant."

"Do you think that changes anything for me?"

"I would understand if it did."

His hands cradle my face. I look into his eyes, the brown eyes I've loved for so long. "Do you want to leave with me? Do you want to put this all behind you?"

"Yes."

He leans down and kisses me again. "I love you, Naila. This changes nothing."

I feel light-headed, shaky. As though I'm slowly waking from a dream. Just maybe, this time will be different. Just maybe, I can be free.

After all the times I tried and failed, can I finally put this nightmare behind me?

Chapter 48

The tiles feel cool on my bare feet. I slip on my sandals and stand outside on the balcony. Back home in Florida, reliable air-conditioning and heating systems made the weather not as big of a deal as it is here. Here, in Pakistan, under the sweltering sun and with the constant blackouts that leave homes and stores without electricity for hours, the weather plays a real role in my life. It is closely felt. I feel today's cool breeze against my face and am grateful in one breath for the change and, in the next, realize sharply that I've now lived in Pakistan long enough to see the weather begin to change. Soon a season will pass me by.

But at least now I know it will be my last season here.

I sit back and remember my encounter with Saif just two days ago. He told me how Carla has been beside herself with grief, urging Saif to join her in circulating a petition to bring me back. I laughed, a tear escaping as I thought of her. It seemed impossible to believe I could ever go back to a life like that.

"You know I'm different now, Saif," I told him. "I might not be the person you remember. Maybe when we get back, you'll see we've grown apart."

"If we've grown apart, we'll find our way back to each other. Trust me. We will," he replied.

We talked until I realized hours had passed. I leapt up. "I have to go back in! They could be up any minute."

"What do you mean?" He looked at me, astonished. "Let's go. Let's go now. My uncle can come as soon as tomorrow morning to take us to the embassy."

"I can't leave now. It'll be time for morning prayers soon. People will be up and about. They'll see us. Look at me, I'm not even wearing a chador."

"But we're not far, just a thirty-minute walk from where I'm staying."

"Saif," I gently told him, "I can't just go stay at some stranger's house with you and wait for your uncle to come."

"Why not? It'll just be for a little bit. We can pay him a little more for his silence. There's nothing a little money can't help."

"I doubt money will make them feel better about harboring me. Once I go missing, everyone in a twenty-five-mile radius will be looking for me, including my uncle. And no amount of money will be worth crossing him."

Just then, a thought occurred to me. "How about Friday? We're invited to a dinner party. I'll get out of it. I'll pretend to be sick, and when they leave, I will leave too. By the time they realize what happened, we'll be far away from here. Then we can go. Besides," I reminded him, "Friday gives me time to get the gold jewelry my parents gave me for the wedding from where it's stored."

And write a letter to Amin, I thought, so he could read it one day and perhaps understand what happened. It would feel wrong, leaving without explaining to him what happened.

I make my way downstairs and into the kitchen. I take in the eggshell walls and wide cabinets. Soon this will just be a part of my memories. Soon I will be free.

I pull out a tea bag from a small glass jar as the teakettle slowly steams on the stovetop. As I pull out a ceramic teacup, I hear the sound of a child's cries down the hallway.

I walk to Feiza's room and knock on her door. She opens it, her hair unkempt, her eyes bloodshot.

"What is it, Feiza? What's the matter?"

"It's Zaina." She ushers me inside.

Zaina lies in the center of the bed, wrapped in a blue blanket. Her face is red and warm, her eyes tightly closed.

"I don't know what to do." Feiza wrings her hands. She presses a wet towel to Zaina's forehead. "She was fine yesterday, a little quieter than usual, but this morning when I went to check on her, she was shivering, and this rash, it seems to be spreading. I don't know what happened."

"What's the matter?"

It's Saba. She wears a blue ruffled outfit and stands at the edge of the bed. Yawning, she rubs sleep from her eyes.

"I've been hearing noises from this room all night," she says. "I could barely close my eyes before she started crying again."

The teapot begins whistling in the distance. "Let me turn that off. I'll be right back." I hurry to the kitchen.

I turn off the stove and place the teapot on a cool burner when I hear Saba's voice behind me. "I need you to do something. Zaina just threw up. Feiza is going to clean it up, and I'll make something to help with the vomiting, but we need to get the fever down. Go to the pharmacy. It's near the small bookstore I took you to the other day. Get her the children's Tylenol. I heard a while ago they had a large order of it in. It's expensive, but nothing else is working."

I clench the money in my hand and walk up to the pharmacy counter, relieved no one else is ahead of me in line. The pharmacist shuffles over to me and nods when I ask for the Tylenol. He's an elderly man with a stooped back who also sells prayer rugs and rosary beads in the adjacent store. Bringing me the medicine I need, he wordlessly slides it across the counter. Counting out the money, I hand it to him before stepping outside.

I look around at the street. A handful of people mill about. Just then, I notice the tonga vala with his dark beard and spiraling mustache. He's reclined in his cart. His eyes are closed. His horse, too, looks asleep. Twenty minutes. That's how long it took me to walk here. I count out my change. Zaina needs the medicine as soon as possible. The tonga will cut the time in half.

I walk up to him, but before I can even speak, his eyes spring open and he looks down at me. He nods as I climb into the back of his wooden cart.

The brown horse clips against the brown road, kicking up dust as it trots. I watch small children, barefoot with toothy grins, chasing the tonga as it slowly picks up speed. Sometimes the older ones manage to jump on, grasping the edge for a little while before leaping off. I wonder where I'll be when the youngest ones chasing the cart now are old enough to leap onto this cart.

Suddenly the tonga jerks to the left. I slide to the edge of the cart. Straightening up, I turn to see that someone has jumped into the cart. Not a child, though—this is a grown person. I gasp. It's Saif.

"Array!" The tonga vala brings his horse to an abrupt stop and glares at Saif. "What do you think you are doing?"

"Maaf kijiye," apologizes Saif. He reaches into his kamiz and pulls out his wallet, handing him a thick wad of bills.

"Where are you going?" His indignant expression changes to one of confusion as he counts the money in his hands.

"Just a few more paces," says Saif. "I'll jump off when I reach where I need to go."

The man looks at the money and then at me hesitantly. "It's okay?" he asks.

I stare at Saif, and then the anxious tonga vala. I nod. The man, visibly relieved, turns around, stuffing the money into his pocket. The horse resumes its steady trot. Familiar homes pass along the way. Saif looks out the other side of the carriage.

"Naila, I need to see you tonight. We need to talk."

Children play soccer in the street. They scatter as the tonga approaches. Barefoot toddlers stare at us. An elderly lady with a hunched back walks slowly out of her house, leaning on a cane.

I feel sick.

"You have no idea the risk you are putting me in," I say through clenched teeth. "This isn't like back home. We can't just sit here together without people noticing."

"It can't wait until Friday. Please meet me outside tonight."

"Okay." I keep my eyes fixed away, looking out at the homes passing by. I hear a thud. The tonga is suddenly lighter. Saif is quickly out of sight.

"Good," Nasim says when I enter the bedroom. She takes the medicine from me. Feiza lifts Zaina up from the bed, and Nasim gives her the medication.

"Give it thirty minutes," she tells Feiza once Zaina is lying back down. "The fever will break. All little ones get sick—she'll be just fine."

"Thank you so much." Feiza hugs me once Nasim leaves. "She's never gotten sick like this before. I completely panicked."

"I know it's scary, but she's going to be okay." I gently squeeze her arm.

She sits next to me at the edge of the bed. We watch Zaina sleeping, her cheeks flushed, her breathing pronounced.

"How are you doing?" Feiza asks softly. "Adjusting better? You seem distracted lately. Getting homesick again?"

I look down at my lap. "I'm fine," I tell her.

"I know how it is. Missing your family. I think I need to visit my parents soon. Spend a few weeks with them," Feiza says. "I'm so tired lately, and I just found out Usman isn't coming back for at least another month."

"You should go visit them. You haven't seen them since I've been here. I'm sure they are missing you and Zaina."

"I know. And they're just an hour away by car." She smiles at me. "It gets easier with time, but no matter how long you are married, you always miss your parents."

I drape an arm around her shoulder and give her a hug. But I don't say anything. I don't trust what I might say.

I lie in bed that night, waiting. I hear footsteps, and then slowly the house sinks into silence. Standing up, I slip outside and make my way to the kitchen. I undo the lock. My heart pounds in my chest; the emotions, carefully pent up all day, now threaten to suffocate me completely, and my armor comes undone.

"I can't believe you," I tell him as soon as I see him. "Do you know what a huge risk you took? Us being seen together?"

"I know. I'm sorry. But it couldn't wait." He runs a hand through his hair. "It's just that, since yesterday, people have started acting strange around us. Or, well, more strange. They've been watching us from the start, but it used to be friendly, curious looks. Now they're asking questions. I'm used to it," he hurriedly assures me. "But today, my dad got stopped by three people, and they had a lot of questions about why we were here and a lot of questions about me." He grinds his foot into the dirt. "And the numberdaar, we're paying him generously, but today he asked us when we're leaving. I'm sure he will let us stay longer if we pay him enough, but we need to go. My dad is really worried. He's trying to reach my uncle so we can leave as soon as possible."

"When?"

"We're not sure about the exact timing yet, but sometime tomorrow for sure, hopefully first thing in the morning. As soon as my dad reaches my uncle, we'll know better, but that's why I came. You need to come with me now so we can be ready to leave as soon as he arrives."

"Hopefully tomorrow morning?" I repeat. "Saif, once I'm missing, the first person Nasim will call is my uncle, and then there's no way of getting out peacefully." I take his hand and hold it in mine. "The people hosting you might be nice, they might really need the money, but trust me, no one will want to harbor us once they know who is looking for them. I'm so sorry you're getting harassed, and your poor father, I can't ever thank him enough for doing all this for me, but leaving now only makes things worse. It's worth it to wait one extra day so we can leave and stay gone. I can't get caught again, Saif. I can't."

"Okay." He sighs. "I'll talk to my dad. He won't be happy, but we'll stick to the plan. Friday after the sun sets."

I hug him. "I wish it could be different, but there's no other way. Not if we can't leave immediately. Just stay indoors. Don't step out of the house until it's time to leave." I kiss him. "Friday will be here before you know it."

Chapter 49

Dinner consists of chicken pulao and minced meat shami kebobs. I love these dishes, but today I can't even pretend to eat. I place the dirty dishes in the sink and turn on the water. Tomorrow night, Amin will be back. I will see him, pretend all is well, and then I will be gone. It's what I want. It's what I deserve. And yet, now that it's almost here, I feel a little nauseous.

As I dry one of the plates with a towel, I'm startled to see Saba standing at the edge of the counter, watching me. She smiles at me widely, like the Cheshire cat.

My heart skips a beat. I pick up another plate, rinsing it under the water. Her eyes bore into me. *What did I do now?* I wonder. Dinner went smoothly. *Did I behave rudely without realizing?* If I did, Saba will certainly let me know. I brace for the evaluation, but Saba simply stares at me in silence.

"Is everything okay, Saba?" I finally ask.

"I just had a question. Did you have trouble finding the pharmacy yesterday?"

"No, I had no trouble finding it. Was I gone too long?"

"No trouble at all?" Saba moves closer. "I heard you had trouble finding the place."

"You heard?"

"Yes. I heard." Her smile grows, spreading across her face. Her eyes dance. "Then I heard you got quite lucky and met someone who showed you how to get there."

"Saba, I never got lost, so that never happened. Nobody showed me how to get there. I went to the pharmacy by myself."

"Well, it's what I heard."

"I've gone to the pharmacy before, so I remembered exactly where it was. I guess whoever told you I was lost was misinformed." I'm moving away from her when I feel a tight grip on my elbow.

Standing inches from me, she leans in. Her previously amused expression is now replaced with one of contempt. "Let's clear something up. I am not as stupid as you might think."

"I don't think you're stupid."

"Then stop the act."

What does she think she knows? I push out a moment of panic. Does she know about the pregnancy? Because I didn't eat dinner? Stay calm, I tell myself. This is the same girl who accused me of stealing money from Nasim's bedroom several weeks earlier. I'm growing tired of the constant snide remarks. Why can't she let me be? I'm not going to let her intimidate me anymore. Gripping the sink, I force myself to meet her gaze. "What is it that you understand? I'd love to clear up any misunderstanding that seems to have you so upset with me."

"That's the thing. There is no misunderstanding, and if you think I will keep it to myself, you are very mistaken."

Before I can respond, Saba simply walks away.

"Naila."

I look over. It's Feiza. Her face is pallid.

"What's wrong?"

She puts a finger over her mouth and motions me toward her bedroom.

I follow her inside and watch her press her ear against the closed door before she grips the lock and fastens it.

"We need to talk," she whispers. "Is it true?"

"Is what true?" My stomach sinks. I don't need to ask. I see her expression. I know.

"I'm just going to say it. I'm not going to run around it." She takes a breath. "Saba came to me a little bit ago. She wanted me to go with her to talk to Nasim. She says you are having an affair. She says she saw you with a man."

I move to speak, but nothing comes out.

"I know, Naila—I'm sure it's just Saba being Saba,"

she says. "You know her, always causing trouble. When do you have time to do anything of any sort? It's the new man she's talking about, I think. The one who's been in town. We saw him at the market, remember? He's wandering about, doesn't talk to anyone. Sometimes he's with another man, an older one, but no one has ever seen them before. People are always trying to find some new story to spin. I just don't understand why she would spin you into it. She doesn't realize that your reputation is now tied with ours—Naila? Are you okay?"

My breath is coming out in gasps. My shoulders tremble.

"Naila," she exclaims, "it's not true, right? She's lying, right?"

"I don't know what to tell you. Whatever I say, no one will believe me."

"I will believe you. Just tell me it's not true. Tell me what's happening. A lot is at stake."

I squeeze my hands together tightly until my knuckles are white.

"Whether what Saba is saying is true or people just believe it to be true, there really is no difference. It won't be good," Feiza says urgently. "Why would she say such a thing?"

"'Won't be good'? Nothing has been good for as long

as I can remember now." I rub my temples as Feiza stares at me in disbelief. "Feiza, I'm going to tell you what is really happening. It seems I no longer have a choice."

With a trembling voice, I tell her everything. About Saif. About my marriage.

Feiza presses a hand against her mouth. "I should have known. We all took it as a cultural thing, the way you just seemed so strange when you first moved here. We thought it was about you being from America, maybe you were homesick or maybe you didn't like us. But I should have figured it out. I should have known something like this had happened."

"You had no way of knowing. None of you had any idea. I realized that soon. How could you know why I was sad?"

"Sad." She lets out a bitter laugh. "Life is full of sadness. It's part of being a woman. Our lives are lived for the sake of others. Our happiness is never factored in. Do I want this life? Living here and seeing my husband a few times a year, raising my daughter alone? I don't know what it was like for you in America, but this is how life is. This is reality. But this advice is coming too late. It's meaningless now."

"I just need until tomorrow evening," I tell her. "Can't I figure out a way to get her to stay quiet for just that long?"

"Gossip spreads faster than kerosene fire," Feiza says. "If she doesn't say it, who knows who else might."

"But I have no place to go." A tear slips down my cheek. "Maybe I should just tell Amin. He gets in first thing tomorrow."

"Tell him?" Feiza says. "And then what?" There's an edge to her voice I have never heard before. "You think he'll press a hand on your head and give you his blessings? You're not his child, Naila. You're not some distant cousin. You're his wife. You think you're going to tell him and he's going to help you pack your things? You honestly think he'll help you? You have no idea what might happen."

I stare at her. I remember the conversation from three months ago. When he learned the nature of our marriage. When he asked me if I wanted to leave. When he said it was too late.

"If Saba knows," Feiza says, "then soon everyone in this house will know. And Nasim, she's going to call your uncle. Amin might stop her if he can. But you know her. And you know your uncle. You're not safe here anymore." She stands up. "I don't know what to say. I wish I could help you. But I should go. I have to be careful too. If I'm seen talking to you, when Nasim realizes I knew and said nothing . . ." Her eyes glisten. She wordlessly walks out of the room.

Chapter 50

I spend the night staring out the window, trying to think of options, alternatives, but nothing comes to mind. My heart sinks when the pink tint of morning arrives. The house is still silent.

No one knows. Yet.

I pace the house. Amin should be home in the morning. Saba hasn't said anything to her mother. She's waiting for Amin, I'm sure. She wants to be the one to tell him. I need to stall her for just today. I need to not leave Amin's side, so she has no chance to corner him.

I hear a dull thud. The sound of a car door shutting outside. I move to the foyer just as the front door creaks open. It's Amin. He steps in, fresh-faced and smiling in a gray suit and blue tie. I catch his gaze, and he smiles. My stomach hurts knowing what I must say. Before either of us can speak, the clatter of plates reverberates through the house.

"Beta," Nasim exclaims, pushing past me to embrace him.

"Ami." He laughs, trying to disentangle himself from her tight hug. "I was gone for less than a week."

"It's not easy for a mother when both her sons are away." She wipes a tear from her eye.

He looks over at me and shakes his head apologetically.

"You're finally home."

It's Saba. She walks up to join us but stands at a distance. Her arms are crossed. Her lips curl for a second, and she opens her mouth to speak when we hear loud shrieks of laughter. Zaina runs into the foyer and topples into Amin's arms. I watch Amin lift her up and toss her in the air. Zaina laughs until her face flushes red.

"The puris are fresh," Nasim announces. "Let's go while they're still hot."

I look at Saba. She is eager to tell him. I can see how she's trying to catch Amin's eye.

I won't last until tonight. I need to talk to him first.

After breakfast, I follow him to the bedroom.

"I feel like I was gone a month!" He turns to me. "It's good you didn't come." He loosens his tie. "We spent the whole time in and out of meetings. I don't even know if Karachi has a sun." He laughs until he sees my drawn expression.

"What's the matter?"

I take a deep breath. Looking at him, I suddenly feel shaky. He told me once he wouldn't help me, but that was before. He knows me now. I can tell in the way he looks at me, the way he defends me from his sister, he loves me. And yet I know that love does not stop people from hurting one another. I know love does not guarantee he can do what I want to ask him to do.

But what other choice do I have?

There's a knock at the door. "What are you two doing?" It's Nasim. "Ruqaya and her husband are here. Don't be rude."

"I'll be out in a minute," he calls. He turns to me with an apologetic smile. "Sorry, you know my mother, she—"

The door handle shakes.

He lets out a deep breath. "I'm sorry. It'll probably only be a half hour."

I watch him press his hand on the doorknob and open it. I look up at the clock. It's noon. Please stay longer than thirty minutes, I pray. Stay all day. I have eight hours to go. Then I'm free.

"Please come visit us again," Nasim says.

Ruqaya and her husband are in the foyer putting their shoes on. After the disastrous encounter with her sister,

Nasim staved off most guests, but now, guests come regularly. Ruqaya, who stands before me, struggling to clasp the tops of her black shoes, is still my favorite. Despite my frequent attempts, she knows little beyond "hello" and "good-bye," but that does nothing to diminish her enthusiasm for learning English.

"Okay," she says now, her face scrunched up in concentration. "I will. See you. Later."

I pretend to smile. I have no time for this today. Today I need to figure out what to do.

Nasim shuts the door after they leave and locks it. "Do you have to teach English to everyone you meet?" She rolls her eyes. "How about practicing your Urdu while you're still in Pakistan?"

Just then I hear the sound of footsteps stomping past me. "Feiza," Saba calls out, "I need to talk to you."

"I'm about to put Zaina down for a nap."

The footsteps continue, faster, and then a door shuts in the distance.

I get up, my heart pounding. I walk quietly down the hallway until I am in front of Feiza's room. I hesitate before pressing my ear to the door.

"Feiza, why won't you believe me?"

"Saba, maybe someone did just need a ride on the tonga. Why should we assume the worst, especially of someone in our own family?"

"I saw him three different times! He's been lurking around. What is he here for? I've heard he won't take his eyes off of her when he sees her. I know it's not just a rumor!"

"So, Saba, what are you saying? That all the men who stare at us know us? That there are secrets behind each look?"

"You know that's not what I'm saying. Something is going on. No one has ever seen this man before here. And haven't you noticed how strange she's been acting lately? The way she just daydreams during dinner? The way she seems lost in thought all the time?"

"Saba, she's always been quiet. It doesn't mean anything."

"I'll let my brother and mother decide what it means. First thing, as soon as I have both of them in front of me, I'm telling them what I know."

"Don't do this," Feiza pleads. "She will have no place to go. You know what will happen if you say something. Think about what you're doing. She'll be sent back, and then her uncle? He'll kill her. You know he will. Don't do this."

Beads of sweat form on my forehead. My mouth goes dry. I back away from the door.

A moment later, Saba emerges. I watch her walk to her bedroom. She slams her door.

I hear the creak of pipes through the walls. Amin is showering. I look at Saba's door and hesitate for a moment before making my way there. Maybe she is the key. I have to stall her long enough to give me a few more hours. Just until the evening comes. Without knocking, I step inside.

"We need to talk."

Saba looks up, genuinely surprised. She is in bed, a book in her lap. I take a deep breath. Each word must be spoken with a full appreciation of its consequences.

"Saba, I know you don't like me, but I wanted to talk to you about what you said to me the other day, what you thought you knew——"

"Thought? I know what I know. If you came here to try to convince me otherwise——"

"I know what you want to do, but you don't know all the facts. Please don't do something you will regret." I walk closer to her and close my eyes. I don't want to do this. I don't want to tell her this.

"Saba, I'm pregnant."

My jaw clenches. I see Saba's blank expression.

"Pregnant?" An amused look spreads across her face.

"Yes. I wanted to tell you so you would think carefully before you decided to say anything to anyone. Especially things that aren't true. There is a lot at stake."

"Pregnant! That is wonderful news." She places her book to the side and stands up. "I'm just curious, though. Who is the father?"

I gasp. "Saba! Who do you think?"

She raises her hands in the air. "Easy, now. It's a simple question—no need to get defensive. How am I supposed to know? It's funny, though . . ." She trails off as she now looks at me. "No one told me you were pregnant. That's the sort of news I would have heard by now, unless of course you were keeping it a secret."

"I wasn't sure I was until recently. That's the only reason."

"So my dear brother does not even know? You haven't told a soul, but you're telling me?"

I hoped by talking to Saba, she would understand, but now, as I look at Saba's smile, I realize there will be no mercy.

Chapter 51

The call to prayer can be heard in the distance. I close my eyes. I try to take in the melodic voice as it resonates through the loudspeakers of the minaret. I consider praying. I yearn for peace, but my heart beats too quickly. My mind races with all the different possibilities. Peace is elusive.

It's been hours since I spoke to Saba. So far she hasn't said a word. Still, I know reprieve is temporary. I feel like prey, hunted and caught, toyed with until the time is right. I try to imagine what will happen when Saba tells everyone. I shudder. What will they do? Will it even matter that I'm Amin's wife? Will it matter that I'm carrying Nasim's grandchild?

I think of my chacha. Does he know about the rumors of my affair? What will he do when he does?

I take a deep breath, trying to still my nerves. I watched Amin minutes earlier, but he was in the kitchen playing with Zaina while Nasim cooked dinner. I was going to call his name, remind him I needed to talk to him, but Feiza's words made me pause. What if she's right? What if going to him will make things worse? What if the best recourse is to say nothing and hope Saba waits until tomorrow to break the news?

My small bag is packed. My wedding gold, some money, some dried fruit to last us a few days if we need it. I never found my passport, but we can deal with that when we have to, when we're far away from here. When we're safe. I think of Saif and shudder. I hope he listened to me and is safely indoors.

Suddenly, I freeze.

There is a man's voice, but it is laced with too much anger to be Amin. The voice comes from a distance. I walk into the dining room. Down the hallway. I hear the voice again.

It is Amin.

"I will not tolerate it! I will not!" Nasim's voice grows louder.

I press my back against the foyer wall.

I can see Amin's face now. He steps into the kitchen in the distance. Saba trails behind; she looks furious.

"What kind of magic has she done on you? Why won't you listen to what we're trying to tell you? You are going to take her word over mine? Your sister's?"

"Ami, Saba. You both have hated her since she came here. You never gave her a chance. I don't care if there are rumors, it doesn't make them true! There are new rumors every day. People talk about it and then they move on. You would say anything to turn me against her."

"Turn you against her?" Saba yells. "Do you hear yourself? I'm your sister, and I am telling you she is having an affair under your nose, and you are accusing us?"

"I don't care if the rumors are true," Nasim interrupts. "Everyone is talking, Amin. They're laughing at us! Don't you care what is happening to our family?"

Saba walks away from the kitchen. Before I can move, she spots me. Her eyes meet mine for a brief moment. They are filled with venom.

"Why don't you ask her for yourself?" She points to me. "Maybe then you will see we're not liars!"

I watch Amin emerge. Nasim is steps behind him. Amin's eyes are red, his face flushed. Looking at me, his eyes soften.

"I'm so sorry." He takes a step toward me. "I don't know what is going on here. Everyone has just lost their minds. It's the only explanation."

Saba walks past him and up to me, her eyes narrow.

"So have you told him yet? All the things you confessed to me?" Before I can respond, she turns to Amin. "Did you know your wife was pregnant?"

Amin stares at my stomach. Looking up at me, he swallows. "Pregnant?"

"Wasn't important enough to tell your husband?" says Nasim with a triumphant expression. "I can't imagine why you wouldn't tell him or us this wonderful news unless you had something to hide."

"Naila . . ." He stares at me. "Is it true?"

I struggle to find my voice. I've seen this scene unfolding since Saba threatened me, and yet now that it's here, I don't know how to begin.

"Amin. Yes. But can we talk in private? I can explain everything to you."

"Why didn't you tell me?" His face is white like paper.

"Look, let's just go to our room. Please, let's go to our room, let's talk—"

"No, there's no more talking in private," Nasim says. "I knew what you were for a very long time, but you've revealed your true colors to everyone, including my son, all on your own now."

"Amin"—my voice trembles—"it's not what you think. If you just talk to me, I can explain to you. I didn't do anything that they're accusing me of. I swear it."

Nasim walks up to me. Her face is inches from mine. I can feel her heavy breathing, see the perspiration forming on her forehead. "Feiza, get her things." She doesn't take her eyes off of me.

"Ami, please—"

"Don't you dare say anything. You do what you are told this minute."

Feiza looks at me and then, lowering her face, her lips quivering, she walks away.

"Amin." I look at him. "Let me explain. You owe me this much."

"Is it true you were on a tonga with a man? Talking with him?" Amin rubs his temples. "Did you know him?"

"Yes." I walk up to him. "Let me explain it to you in private. It's not the full story. And this pregnancy . . . it's yours."

Amin lets out an empty laugh. "How can it be mine? Is that even possible?"

"It is." I stare at him. "How can you, of all people, question that?"

His expression pales.

Nasim's eyes are fiery. "You see? She knows him! You heard her, Amin! You know now we are not liars? And look at her! Admitting all of this, and instead of pleading for mercy, she talks to you like this?" She turns to me.

"After everything we have done for you, you try to ruin us? I'm done being nice to you. You are worth less than the dirt on the ground I walk on, and now everyone sees it."

I look at Amin. He looks back at me. I see the unspoken accusations on his lips.

I feel sick. Somewhere deep down, I had hoped Amin cared about me. That he would help me. But now, I realize, he will not intercede.

"You want me to leave, and I want to go," I tell them. I watch Saba take the suitcase from Feiza. Green and blue pieces of fabric poke through the latch. "I'll just take my suitcase and leave. You will never hear from me again." I pull away, but Nasim yanks me by the arm, her nails digging into my skin.

"You would like that, wouldn't you? No, you will leave on our terms. Everyone is going to know we cast you out." She turns to Feiza. "Call her uncle. Tell him to come get her. She'll be waiting outside," Nasim says.

"Amin." Tears stream down my face. Nasim drags me by the arm. "Give me a chance to explain myself. You owe me this much after everything."

"But you never told me." His voice rises. "You turned me into a fool in my own home. You lied to me." Shaking his head. "All this time, I always defended you."

"I didn't do anything!"

"Things are out of my hands now. They are beyond what I want, and what I can do. I can't help you now. It's too late."

Saba's hands shove me down the hallway and outside. The sun shines brighter than usual in the sky. A burst of air churns a patch of sand and blurs my vision; the heat of the road burns my bare feet. Grabbing the suitcase, Nasim throws it onto the dusty road. The force swings it open on impact. My clothes litter the street in blues, whites, and pastels.

"You think you can live in my house and deceive us?" Nasim walks up to me. Her face is flushed, power now squarely back in her hands. "How dare you take advantage of my kindness and ruin my family name?" I feel a blistering slap across my face. The force tilts my head back. I taste blood against my tongue. "I have an unmarried daughter in my house, and you bring shame to my family? You sully my name?" Nasim shoves me hard. I fall forward, tripping against the concrete step, my foot twisting when I land with a thud.

Nasim seems possessed by a demon. I try covering myself from Nasim's feet—she kicks me with each curse. I try turning inward, but it's no use.

I can make out people, a small crowd. They surround

us. Small children, neighboring women, some who even came over to the house, who patted my hands as they thanked me for the tea I made them. They stand now at the edges, shaking their heads, whispering, watching.

How long has it been?

I no longer feel pain. It is as though I am floating above my body, watching events transpire on a screen. I'm numb as blood trickles down my nose, settling into my swollen lip. I think of my brother, my childhood bed with lace ruffles on the edges; I think of Saif, his dimple, his lips warm and soft, pressed against mine, the stubble tickling my cheeks. I feel a shadow, the world darkening, as I wait for everything to go black.

I wait for the next blow, but then—nothing. I hear voices. Looking up, I see Nasim; her body is suddenly yanked backward. Amin has pulled her off of me.

I try sitting up but wince—my wrists sear with pain. Just then, Amin's gaze shifts. His jaw hardens.

"Who is that? Is that him? What the hell do you think you're doing here?" Amin shouts at someone marching toward us.

It's Saif, but Amin doesn't wait for an answer. Before I can process any more, Amin charges him.

I bite my lip and push myself up through the pain, but before I can do anything, Amin shoves Saif to the ground.

Who is this person? I can scarcely recognize Amin right now as he punches Saif.

I don't pause to think. I don't pause to reflect on consequences of any kind. Before anyone can move, I'm on my feet. Anger rises in me. It propels me.

"Stop." A loud voice—my voice—stops Amin in his tracks.

He looks up at me. His breathing is rapid. He takes me in, but he hasn't moved. I've never seen him so furious.

"I didn't choose this, Amin. You know that. You know I don't belong here. And you know you will be happier with someone else. What are you getting out of hurting him? What good can possibly come of any of this? Do you want to keep us here long enough for my uncle to get here and finish what you've started?"

Just like that, my words seem to deflate him. The rage in his eyes evaporates. I watch his shoulders slump. Something in him fades.

Just then, we hear the screech of tires. A car door slams. A yellow car pulls up just a few feet away. The brake lights glow red. A door opens, and Saif's father jumps out.

"Let's go," he shouts, walking quickly toward us.

Saba's eyes are large and round. She takes a step toward us. Nasim follows. They are marching up to us.

Saif stands up and walks over to me. He places an arm

around my waist, helping me to fully stand. My foot throbs, but I no longer feel any pain.

"Are we putting on a circus act for all to see? What is this?" Nasim demands.

"This is us leaving," I tell her.

"After everything she's put us through, she just leaves?" Saba cries out.

"No," Nasim says, her eyes never leaving mine. "She does not get to humiliate us this publicly and then just run off." She takes a step toward me. "Over my dead body."

"Enough," Amin says.

His voice is quiet, but it silences them both. I wipe dirt mingled with blood from my face and look at him.

"Leave them alone," he finally says. "Let them leave in peace."

I look at him, and something inside me hurts. I want to tell him so many things. But I know that it's now too late.

Saif and his father help me walk to the car. I get inside, and Saif sits next to me. I look back at the house of cement and bricks, the gravelly path leading to the door. Feiza stands at the entryway, holding Zaina tightly to her. My chest compresses when I see them. Zaina watches me with large eyes. The car jerks forward, turns right, and then, after so many months, after everything I've been through—they're all gone.

"Are you okay?" Saif asks softly. "We'll be home before you know it."

I rest my head on Saif's shoulder and close my eyes. I have gone to hell and back, but I'm okay. Finally, I am home.

Epilogue

I'll get that." Saif races to the stove to turn off the squealing teakettle. I watch him pour the hot water into the ceramic cups with tea bags and cover them as they steep.

"Are you nervous?" He puts an arm around my shoulder and kisses me on the head.

"Yes," I tell him. "I just can't believe they're here. Probably just a few miles away."

"You don't have to do this. I can call them and tell them it's not going to work."

"It's fine." I kiss him. "They can't do anything to me now."

My brother, Imran, called me just last week. My mother is sick. Very sick. And she wants to see me.

"It will be okay." He pulls me into a hug.

It's been two years since I left Pakistan and put my nightmare firmly behind me, but today is the first time I will see them. "Your parents are my parents now," I had told Saif when I first returned. His father helped me sort things out at the American embassy. His mother held me as my body writhed with pain from the loss of my pregnancy, an unexpected grief that lingers to this day. His parents helped arrange the particulars of my divorce. And it was his parents who attended our simple marriage in court two months ago.

My life is different than I would have pictured it, but it's a good life. I love the brick-front apartment just minutes from campus, with its low ceilings and dim lighting. I love my green curtains and the white lights I've strung around its periphery. It's taken me time to work up to it, but this semester, I took my first full schedule. I lost my old scholarship and my spot in the medical program, but I'm thankful for student loans that help me make good on dreams I thought were long gone. Each day I feel more like myself. Each day the past feels more squarely placed where it belongs, behind me.

I look up at the clock on the wall. I don't want to see either of them—but they need to see me now. With Saif. They need to see just how wrong they were.

I look out the window; two figures are approaching the building. The woman wears a green salwar kamiz and a black coat, and her hair is gathered in a graying bun. The man next to her has a bit of a stoop, his glasses thick and black, his hair fully gray now. No hint of black remains.

I close my eyes and take a deep breath. Something inside me suddenly aches.

"You can do this," Saif says.

Any minute now, the doorbell will ring. I close my eyes as a tear slips down my face. Saif squeezes my hand. I look down at his hand and smile. Love is about the good moments, but it's about holding on to each other during the difficult ones too. Coming out the other side, weathered but still holding hands, isn't easy. It's the most difficult thing there can possibly be, but I know now it's the truest test of love there is. Life hasn't been easy, but it gets less painful every day, and as I look at Saif, I know that love—in its essence, at its core—is the most bittersweet thing there is.

Author's Note

When I was twenty-two years old, I married the love of my life. Both Pakistani-Americans raised in traditional families, our wedding was semiarranged by our parents. We met only once, surrounded by family, before getting engaged, and only a handful of times before our wedding day. Though I barely knew him, I trusted my parents and looked forward to getting to know him for the rest of my life. Eleven years and two children later, I am so thankful for the decision I made. It was a leap of faith, but one I am glad I took.

Not all couples, however, are as lucky as we were. Unlike my story—where we were equal partners making a choice to spend our lives together—forced marriages are brought about through coercion, pressure, threats, and sometimes, outright violence.

I personally knew girls, born and raised in the United States, who were pressured or coerced into marriages they never would have chosen for themselves. Because they were taught from very young ages that they would have little to no say in this matter, many grew up believing they could not go against their parents or turn to anyone for help. I've known too many people who have had to deal with abuse, failed marriages, and parents threatening to disown them if they tried to leave.

Naila's story might be fictional, but the reality of forced marriages is unfortunately true for many in America and around the world. While this book is set in Pakistan, the issue is not limited to one particular culture or religion— it is a problem that transcends race and religion, affecting many diverse groups of people. Though every country and religion opposes the practice of forced marriage, it is real, it is dangerous, and it is happening in our own backyard. Many other countries have acknowledged this crisis and expanded their resources—the United Kingdom even has kidnapping rescue units in the most at-risk countries. In the United States, however, forced marriages remain a silent epidemic. It is my hope that this novel, like all good books, will transport readers to a new world, but will also provide a voice for so many girls who see themselves in Naila and who shouldn't have to suffer in silence.

Resources

If you or someone you know needs advice or help, please contact:

The Tahirih Justice Center: Offices in Arlington, Virginia; Baltimore, Maryland; and Houston, Texas. http://www.tahirih.org/contact-us

Unchained at Last: info@unchainedatlast.org or http://www.unchainedatlast.org

US Department of State, Office of Overseas Citizens Services: 1-888-407-4747, or 202-501-4444 if calling from overseas.

Acknowledgments

One thing I've learned on the book journey is just how many people it takes to create any book readers hold in their hands. You do not hold the hard work of a single person, but the heart and soul of all the people who helped make that book a reality.

First and foremost, I am indebted to my amazing editor, Nancy Paulsen, for her incredible insights that helped take my novel to the next level. She is truly gifted at what she does.

Many thanks to Sara LaFleur for her help and guidance and to Lindsey Andrews for the beautiful cover art, as well as the entire team at Nancy Paulsen Books and Penguin Young Readers for all their support along the way.

I hit the jackpot by landing not only an amazing

publishing house and editor but an incredible agent in Taylor Martindale. Many thanks to Taylor for believing in this manuscript from the start and for loving these characters like I do. A simple acknowledgment will never suffice to capture just how appreciative I am for all she's done for me. My gratitude also to Stefanie Von Borstel and the entire team at Full Circle Literary.

When we got married, my husband promised to support me in all my dreams, and I will love him forever for keeping this vow. Thank you for believing in me and for babysitting little ones while I worked on edits. A writer's journey can be an uncertain one, but I stuck with it because of his support every step of the way. Thank you also to our sons, Waleed and Musa, for being a piece of my heart and for being a driving force in all I do.

To my parents, Kalsoom and Anwar Saeed, thank you for the detailed feedback on this novel and for always being so proud of me. To my friends Ayesha Mattu, Sonya Choudry, and Saadia Memon, thanks for being my beta readers and helping me verify research along the way, and many thanks to Russ and Elizabeth Hetzel for being early readers as well. To my brothers, Ali and Aamir, thank you for always encouraging me to follow my dreams, and to all my family and dear friends (you know who you are!), thank you so much for being part of my life.

A very special thanks to Suzanne Staples for giving me feedback when this book was still in its infancy. Her novels featuring Pakistani protagonists showed me my stories mattered and deserved to be told. Thank you for encouraging me and for being my inspiration and mentor.

And last but certainly not least, thank you to Tracy Lopez for being there from the very beginning, when this book was just an idea living inside my head. She was the first person to read this story, and she's been there through every edit and revision along the way. I can never ever thank her enough for all the heart and energy she put into making this the best book it could be. I am forever thankful for her support and her friendship.

GLOSSARY

abu: father

ami: mother

array: hey

beta: literal word for "son," but often used for daughters as well

chacha: father's younger brother

chachi: father's younger brother's wife

chai: tea

charpay: a traditional woven bed

dupatta: scarf

kamiz: long tunic with side seams, often worn with a *salwar*

khala: mother's sister

kulfi: sweet dairy dessert similar to ice cream

lengha: a long skirt worn with a blouse

maaf kijiye: forgive me

mubarak: congratulations

nahin: no

paratha: flat, round buttered bread

phupo: father's sister

rupee: Pakistani currency

salwar: loose pajama-style pants worn by men and women in Pakistan, often with a *kamiz*

sari: an outfit worn by South Asian women that consists of a short blouse and a lengthy cloth draped around the body

sherwani: traditional South Asian male outfit with a long fitted coat worn at weddings and other important occasions

tamasha: spectacle